Very carefully, my eyes never leaving the water in case I saw some dangerous-looking ripples, I pulled the canoe out and put it back on the trolley.

As I rode away I thought I heard soft, whispering laughter, but it seemed to come from my imagination playing tricks on me.

At least I hoped it was my imagination.

the Swampland trilogy

Swampland

Tankworld

Endsville

Swampland

S.R. Martin

POINT

SCHOLASTIC INC.
New York Toronto London Auckland Sydney
Mexico City New Delhi Hong Kong

No part of this publication may be reproduced in whole or in part, or stored in a retrieval system, or transmitted in any form or by any means, electronic, mechanical, photocopying, recording, or otherwise, without written permission of the publisher. For information regarding permission, write to Scholastic Australia Pty Limited, P. O. Box 579, Gosford 2250 Australia.

ISBN 0-439-04393-X

All rights reserved. Published by Scholastic Inc., 555 Broadway, New York, NY 10012, by arrangement with Scholastic Australia Pty Limited. SCHOLASTIC and associated logos are trademarks and/or registered trademarks of Scholastic Inc.

12 11 10 9 8 7 6 5 4 3 2 1   0 1 2 3 4 5/0

Printed in the U.S.A.   01

First Scholastic Trade paperback printing, March 2000

Typeset in 12/15 Bembo.

1

The day the Tuckers moved in was unpleasant, to say the least.

It had been raining steadily for over a week, an endless downpour of freezing cold water which never stopped. To walk out in it (even with the full rigmarole of raincoat, umbrella and wellies) meant you were going to get soaked through.

Everyone's lawn and garden had turned to mush, and even the leaves on the trees had started to fall off. Water found its way through windows and under doors, causing great, spreading stains on the carpet; and you could be excused for thinking that we were all living in slowly decaying life-support modules kilometres under the surface of the ocean.

People simply stopped going outside.

Instead, they sat and watched television for hour upon hour, hoping for some sign of relief from the weather reports.

Even the people who presented the weather were depressed at having to repeat the same thing over and over. It was as if they knew the effect it was having on people and somehow began to take it all to heart, as if it were all their fault.

The highest absentee rates from work and school were recorded.

The suicide rate shot up dramatically.

And then the rain just stopped.

Dead.

At exactly seven-fifteen on the morning of November 25.

I can remember it clearly, because the silence that followed was deafening. Everyone was so used to the rain that it had become like the sound of their own breathing. When it was no longer there it caused a moment of panic as people frantically tried to work out what was missing from their lives.

It was like a sudden pause in the world.

Then after a while you began to hear cheering as people realised what had happened. It was far off to begin with, then more and more voices joined in, and the sound came floating across the backyards as people gradually came outside.

Then the sun came out and it got very, very hot.

Because of the water that had soaked into the soil, the sudden onset of extreme heat created huge amounts of steam, which rose and formed a fog bank about 5 metres high.

I was sitting out on the front step of our house watching the shapes of people, bikes and vehicles swirling in and out of the strange bright clouds of vapour when a Grace Brothers truck pulled up at the house next door. I also noticed that the *For Sale* sign which had been on the front fence for the last six months was no longer there. It must have been taken down sometime during the week of rain while everyone was hiding indoors.

It was like a sauna outside and the three removalists

were already sweating when they got out of the cab of the truck. One of them pounded on the front door but it appeared that no-one, as yet, was inside, so they stood around smoking and looking huge.

There was a key to the house hidden under a fake rock in the back garden. It had been left there when old Mrs Geralitis died. She didn't have any relations, and as far as I could tell my brother and I were the only people who knew about the key. We used to watch her through a hole in the back fence and often saw her take it out of its hiding place. Mrs Geralitis had a bad habit of locking herself out of the house when she went down to the shop for milk or bread. The fake rock looked really natural, so no-one from the real estate agency that was trying to sell the house had noticed it, and after the house had been emptied of all its furniture Zac and I used to sneak in and hoon around in the empty rooms.

This was not as easy as it sounds, as Mrs Geralitis's house is not designed for wheelchairs like ours is, and I had to haul Zac's chair up the back steps then pull him up afterwards.

He used to think it was hilarious, with me huffing and puffing away—I'm not the fittest of fifteen-year-olds—and him hanging there like 'a useless leg of pork', as he habitually called himself when he was out of the chair.

Zac was a couple of years older than me, and definitely a lot fitter and larger, even though what was left of his legs wasn't a whole lot. They'd sort of withered away after the accident, in that weird time when he didn't care what happened to him and none of us knew what to say or do around him. We all did the things we had to, like bathe him and change the bag attached to his leg and everything—Mum and Dad trying to put a good face on it all and me just being sulky about it—but there was this sort of unspoken agreement between us just not to accept that it had happened.

It was our guilty little secret, something that we didn't even admit amongst ourselves.

This went on for about a year, then he suddenly snapped out of it.

One night he went to bed as Zac the zombie, the next morning he was Zac the athlete, scoffing raw eggs for breakfast and propelling himself through the back streets screaming 'Out of the way, bipeds!'

No-one really had an answer to that.

What do you say to a sweaty young bloke in a wheelchair with a crazed look in his eyes?

His upper body became massive from all the exercise he did in that damn chair, whipping around the streets like some maniac in a Formula One racer. He was going to be in the Paralympics, or so he reckoned, and win himself a gold medal.

'That'd really show 'em, wouldn't it? Boy racer in a wheelchair with a gold medal around his neck. Paint the whole bloody wheelchair gold I will,' he used to say to me as I rode along beside him on my bike.

He never blamed anyone for what happened to him, as a lot of people in his position tend to. It would have been futile really. He had stolen the car and had been about as drunk as anyone can get when it rolled. I guess he spent that year admitting it to himself and after that just accepted it, deciding to get on with his life.

Which was a good thing, really, good for all of us. I don't know what Mum and Dad would have turned out like if he'd kept it up much longer. You always read about those sorts of things in the papers, about ordinary people who just snap some night and take a shotgun to their whole family. Not that our family owns a shotgun or anything.

I no longer think about those things as something foreign, as something that could never happen to me.

I've seen murder in my own parents' eyes.

Not an angry, rage-filled kind of murder like you see in the movies, but one born out of tiredness and desperation, one that exists because there's nothing else there to think about anymore.

One inspired by colostomy bags and smeared buttocks and endless hours of depression.

It sort of became our place, Mrs Geralitis's house, in those months before the Tuckers moved in, a place that was our secret.

We'd never really been all that close before the accident, because Zac was always off down the pub with his mates (he's always looked a lot older than he is) or going out with girlfriends, and I sort of had my own crowd as well. Then during that year when he wasn't really himself I guess we got cut off from the people we thought we were close to.

It's amazing how easily it can happen.

His friends stopped coming around to see him after the first few weeks because all he'd do was stare at them. It's not that he didn't recognise them or anything; I just don't think he recognised what they were anymore.

It was like everyone who could walk was from another planet.

And I stopped seeing my friends as well, because all they'd want to do was talk about my big, bad brother, the one who stole cars and got in a chase with the police and ended up as a cripple from the waist down.

I sort of liked it for a while, the notoriety, then I got bored, and then I just started getting angry. All that did was get me beaten half to death, because—as I think I said before—I'm not the fittest of people, and I'm sure as hell no fighter, not like Zac used to be, anyway.

He'd always be coming home with black eyes and skinned knuckles, and his friends always looked to him as the one who'd do the standing up for them if they ever ran into trouble.

Fat lot of standing up for him they did when he was in trouble.

So after he started improving, talking to people and exercising and stuff, we just stuck together.

And then Mrs Geralitis died and we took over her house.

It was strange at first, being in this huge old place with nothing in it except hints of the life that had been there before.

The house had always been something of a mystery to us, as we'd never been inside or anything, just talked to the old lady in the front yard. I think Mum went inside once to help out with some chore or other, and said it was decorated in a Mediterranean style, whatever that means.

No matter what it used to look like, it was completely empty when Zac and I started visiting.

We'd wander from room to room, Zac's wheels making eerie squeaking noises on the old linoleum. You could see where there had been things on the walls, because the paint hadn't faded as much where they'd hung as everywhere else. In one room there was the perfect pattern of three flying ducks; in others the oval or square shapes of picture frames, and Zac reckoned one room had masks on the walls because the shapes left behind reminded him of human heads.

Zac always had an active imagination. I guess that was what got him into trouble.

We made the kitchen our base of operations, because there Zac could lever himself up onto the bench and sit propped back against the wall. It was also on the opposite side from our house, so neither Mum nor Dad would be able to see us through the windows.

He'd sit there barking orders at me while I tried to learn the tricks of his wheelchair.

I always had a fascination with that chair, right from the beginning, and Zac was able to do some amazing wheelstands and things in it—probably the sorts of things he used to do in other people's cars, but I never got around to asking him that.

So every few days we'd spend some time in Mrs Geralitis's deserted kitchen with him trying to teach me how to be a Top Gun wheelchair rider, but I was never anywhere as good as he was. Just wasn't strong enough, I guess.

Then we'd have these wild races through all the empty rooms on a course we had worked out, me on my skateboard and Zac spinning his wheels as fast as his arms could manage. This left some nasty marks on the lino, especially around the corners, and a few long scrapes along the walls where the chair had got too close.

'Don't worry about it,' Zac said to me. 'Whoever moves in here'll spend a fortune on restoring this place anyway. They'll rip up the lino and replaster all the walls, so no-one'll give a stuff about a few marks and scratches.'

He was right, too. They gutted the place eventually, but I'm getting a bit ahead of myself.

The Tuckers finally arrived.

They had two cars, a 911 Porsche and a Volvo station wagon.

There were five of them, but it was a bit hard to tell in the fog what sex each was.

The temperature must have been approaching the early 30s, so the steam was literally pumping out of the ground.

They piled out of the cars, spoke briefly with the removalists and went inside the house. Minutes later, furniture was being unloaded from the van, but I couldn't get an image of what they were like from that either, because everything was wrapped in cardboard.

I'd been watching the unloading for about half-an-hour when I heard some squeaking and a thump on the veranda behind me.

'There goes the neighbourhood,' Zac said, coming to a halt beside me.

'Why's that? You haven't even seen them yet.'

'The Porsche. Only a certain type of person drives one of those, and they're not my favourite type.'

'You'd driven a few in your time, if I remember rightly.'

He grinned down at me and made a swipe at my head. I ducked.

'None of them were mine, though. I'd never own one.'

'Must be fun to drive.'

He looked across at the German car. For a second there his eyes seemed to be very far away, sort of how he looked all the time in that year after the accident. Then he grinned again.

'Yeah, they're fun to drive. But don't go getting any ideas.'

8

I held my hands up in surrender.

'Not me, brother.'

'They've also got a Volvo,' he sneered. 'That makes them even worse.'

'Mum and Dad have a Volvo.'

'Exactly,' he said with finality.

Then he motored down the ramp and headed into the strange half-light of the street.

'Off for my practice. Y'wanna come?'

I shook my head.

'Not today, it's too hot. It'd be like riding through a sauna. You must be half crazy.'

'You can say that again,' he said, rearing back in a sudden wheelstand and taking off down the footpath.

'You must be half crazy,' I whispered after him.

I spent the better part of the morning sitting on the step trying to catch a good look at the Tuckers, but had no success. Everything was too blurred by the fog.

Eventually, four of them came out and left in the Volvo and the father stayed to oversee the workmen.

They finished unloading by about two in the afternoon, but by this time I'd gone inside for lunch. When I came out again the air had almost cleared and the removalist truck was just thundering off down our street.

Mr Tucker was standing by his Porsche. He was extremely tall and very dapper in a light summer suit of some green shimmery material and expensive snakeskin cowboy boots.

As he opened the door he looked up and saw me standing on the veranda. He grinned and waved. I half-waved back at him, then the car burbled off down the street.

And that was my introduction to the Tuckers, though it was a couple of weeks before I got to meet any of them personally. They spent the time living in a hotel in the city while workmen tore out Mrs Geralitis's old bathroom and kitchen and replaced them, sanded back the floorboards throughout the house and replastered the walls.

They did exactly what Zac said they would, and he watched their progress with a permanent sneer attached to his face.

'Yuppies,' he'd mutter to himself, then take off on his morning practice runs (he always called them runs, and I could never work out why—to me they were more like shoves).

Then the big day arrived and the Porsche and Volvo became permanent fixtures in the driveway, and Mrs Tucker and her three daughters filled the reborn house with noise.

I remember it well, because it was the same day that old Marty's dog, Blitz, disappeared. Marty came around to our house that night looking for him, saying Blitz never strayed away and he was worried.

Old Marty had lived in our street longer than anyone. He had a ramshackle place down at the end where the street sort of peters out and becomes swamp. His place would have been the same sort of age as Mrs Geralitis's, but not nearly as grand looking.

The dog was a bitser that had to be my age at least, and you always saw it shuffling along behind Marty when he was out walking. It occasionally made an attempt to chase Zac's chair, but it was so easily outdistanced that he never paid it any attention. I think he kind of liked it, the fact that it was something he could easily beat.

Anyway, we all felt that the dog had probably wandered off and either been run over or bitten by a tiger snake in the swamp somewhere. We all forgot about Blitz, except for the times we saw Marty wandering about calling his name.

A couple of kids found him a week later, way back in the swamp.

Someone had taken two saplings, bent them down to the ground and tied the dog between them.

Then they let them go.

It snapped Blitz cleanly in two, or as cleanly as something like that can.

I can still hear the screams those kids made when they came running out of the swamp. They were only six or seven years old, poor little grommets.

They kept saying something about dogs in trees, but it was only one dog.

Two trees.

***

I suppose it should have been obvious, but I'm the sort of person who deliberately overlooks the obvious because I think there's going to be something more interesting going on behind it. It's a selfish attitude, I know that now, and it's turned around and bitten me right where it hurts the most.

My brother would have said that it serves me right, that I deserve everything I've got and then some. That by being blind to what was right in front of my eyes I put myself and everyone around me in positions that were, at best, unpleasant, if not downright life-threatening.

I was the closest to the heart of the beast and should have understood its intentions.

Zac would have said it, but he's probably dead by now. In some ways that's my fault as well, but he would never have blamed me for it. Zac had a different way of looking at things from everyone else.

But if the truth be known, even if I had seen it, seen right down into its soul and spied the crook-backed thing that drove it, I'm not certain I would have done anything anyway.

Love was involved, you see, or at least infatuation, and that puts a different perspective on things.

She was like something out of an exotic movie, one you'd see on SBS with lots of subtitles and long, lingering looks in shabby rooms.

From the first moment I saw her she was always something foreign to me. I guess this was what the attraction was, that she was unusual and somehow out-of-place in our rather ordinary little neighbourhood, but I can't really be certain of that.

Zac thought my hormones were involved, and that my actions from the moment I met her were therefore not entirely my own.

The doctors who are treating me for burns say that I am still in shock and it will be some time before I see things in a rational manner. (This is what my parents tell me, anyway.) And the psychologist who pops in every morning always nods patiently and smiles as if he understands, but I know they're all just humouring me.

Poor little Marvin, they're all thinking, still frightened and confused by what happened, blaming himself for his brother's death, everything all mixed up in his head like pot luck stew.

Oh, I'm frightened all right, so damn scared I can hardly eat or sleep anymore, but I'm not confused about some things. And I don't blame myself for what happened to Zac. It was my fault, but I don't blame myself. There wasn't a thing I could do about it, and Zac always said to me that you shouldn't ever be guilty about something you have no control over.

I'll always be grateful to him for that.

The doctors say to my parents that all the weight I've lost and the ever-increasing bags of blue under my eyes are the result of trauma, and they're part right. But it's not past trauma that is affecting me, it's still going on as far as I'm concerned.

It's just that the people who know about it are not people I really want to meet.

This much is very clear to me, far clearer than it's ever been before, and the moment I get out of this hospital they won't see me for dust.

I'm going to be so far gone no-one's even going to know I've been.

※※*※*※*

The first time I saw her it was early morning.

I'd been out for a run with Zac and was putting my bike back in the shed when I heard a strange noise from next door.

It sounded like the tinkling of a small bell, but it was almost too faint for me to make out.

Peering through the hole that Zac and I had always used to spy on Mrs Geralitis, I couldn't see anything except the area near the back door, so I made the mistake of climbing up on the fence to have a good look around. Somewhere in the back of my mind I was thinking that it was too early in the morning for anyone except madmen like Zac and me to be out, and that the noise was from some animal, maybe a cat.

I'm not fond of cats, hate them in fact, and was worried that our new neighbours had brought one into the house with them.

As my head rose up over the top of the palings another head rose up to mirror it from the other side, except this head had beams of light flashing from it.

I let out a pathetic little squeak of fear and fell backwards, the force of the fall knocking the breath from my body. I could see hundreds of multi-coloured stars drifting in from the sides of my vision like a distant fireworks display.

As I lay there on the ground trying to breathe I heard laughter and the bell noise again, and when I finally looked up she was already half-way across the fence, her face all aglow with amusement.

'Nice one, chubby,' she laughed at me. 'You look like you've seen something out of Elm Street. Or haven't you ever seen a girl before?'

I'd certainly never seen a girl like her before.

She squatted on her heels, leaned right down over me and sniffed loudly.

'You're a bit on the nose,' she said, still half-laughing.

'I've been out riding with my brother,' I gasped in reply. 'I haven't had my shower yet.'

'He's the good-looking one in the wheelchair with all the muscles isn't he? What's his name?'

'Zac.'

'Uh huh.'

She cocked her head quizzically.

'Zachariah, actually. It's from the Bible. And I'm Marvin,' I continued.

'Marvin?'

'Yeah. After a bloke called Marvin Gaye. He was some sort of famous musician from ages ago.'

'Like Mozart?'

'I suppose so. He's dead anyway.'

'That accounts for it I guess.'

'For what?' I said, struggling up into a sitting position.

'Parents are always giving kids dumb names just because someone's dead.'

'Like?'

'Like Marvin,' she said, and grinned broadly. She had almost-perfect white teeth, but they were a bit too small and pointed for my taste.

Now that I could breathe and the fireworks display had faded away, I began to pay a bit more attention to her appearance.

The flashing lights which had given me such a shock had been caused, I could now see, by sunlight reflecting from all the tiny rings and studs she had stuck through her face. There were innumerable earrings, of different sizes, up and down her ears, studs in her nose and eyebrows, and even one through her lip at the corner of her mouth.

Every time she moved her head she glittered.

The tinkling sound I had heard came from a couple of small bells that were attached to the earrings.

She was about my age and had her blonde hair cut in a short bob around her face. Her eyes were green and seemed to glitter with a constant sense of amusement.

I must have had a funny look on my face because she suddenly stopped smiling.

'What are you staring at, chubby?'

'Nothing. I mean ... well ... all the ummm ... '

I sort of fluttered one hand around my face, not sure of how to describe all the adornment.

'Oh this,' she said. 'Don't you get into any body piercing over here?'

'Well, yes. But maybe not to the same extent. They'd

throw a fit at school, and I don't think my parents would really be into it either.'

She laughed.

'My parents think it's a sign of my creative expression. They're into that sort of thing. I've got a few in places you can't see as well. But I take most of the ones off my face before I go to school.'

She stood up and reached out a hand to me.

'Come on, you look like you've recovered.'

Her grip felt like it broke most of the small bones in my hand, and she seemed to lift me up off the ground like I weighed nothing at all. Even though she was only my height she seemed incredibly strong.

'I like to jog in the mornings,' she continued, 'so maybe I can join you and your brother sometime.'

'Yeah, fine. But we move pretty fast, you know. We're on wheels.'

'I know,' she said and swung herself back up over the fence like it wasn't there at all.

'Be seeing you,' she called as she dropped out of sight.

I stood staring at the space she'd vacated and had the strangest feeling that I'd just experienced something that wasn't quite real.

Her head suddenly reappeared and the feeling immediately went away.

'It's Edith, by the way. My name. But you can call me Edie. Named after some depressing singer my mother likes to listen to. She's dead as well.'

I was pretty sure she didn't mean her mother.

After she had disappeared again I stood and stared at the fence for some time.

I couldn't quite put my finger on what the feeling was I experienced each time her head dropped below the level of the fence. It was almost like what I thought I had experienced had never really occurred.

There was a distinct feeling of loss, though, of an emptiness that needed to be filled.

But I knew I'd be seeing more of her, a lot more. If for no other reason than we were both named after dead singers. It was like a sign that we were destined to be together in some way.

I shook my head and went inside for a shower.

As we were in the long holiday break, Zac and I had a project planned. For months now I had been wanting a canoe so that I could go exploring deep into the swamp.

When I say deep, I mean into those areas I couldn't reach by foot. It's not as if we're talking the Everglades here. Our swamp was only a few acres in size and bounded by a main highway on the opposite side from our housing subdivision. You could walk around the whole thing in an hour, so it wasn't as if I was going off to be Doctor Livingstone or anything; you couldn't really get lost in there. Not lost for any length of time, anyway. But there were some fairly inaccessible areas which could only be reached by something that travelled on water, and this was where I wanted to go.

Some time back a few of us had got together and built what could loosely be described as a raft from some 44-gallon drums, old planks and mismatched pieces of rope we'd salvaged from everyone's fathers' sheds. We'd also fashioned some long poles from tree branches which we used to push it in the general direction we intended to go.

Everything seemed to work fine. To begin with, anyway.

There were three of us: Max, Michael and myself. We used to refer to ourselves as the Triple Ms.

Zac used to call us M & M & Ms, and say we were all full of a chocolatey substance.

We had to actually build the raft in the water, otherwise we'd have never got it off the bank; it was far too heavy. When it was completed we pushed off and poled ourselves, rather clumsily until we got the hang of it, into what we considered to be uncharted territory.

And it was exciting, none of us have ever denied that, though Max and Michael will never go back in there again after what happened.

You see, the day was fairly sunny when we started our expedition, but as we got deeper and deeper into the swamp it became quite overcast. So from travelling through an area of dripping paperbarks and sparkling green waterways filled with tadpoles and frogs, we were suddenly plunged into gloom and shadows and our imaginations became a little overextended.

Max had always been an addict of old films like *The Creature from the Black Lagoon* and *It Came from under the Sea*, so it didn't take an awful lot to get him going. And Michael and I were rather fond of things like *Nightmare on Elm Street*.

The deeper we travelled into the swamp, the darker it became, and eventually it began to rain.

Heavily.

Then we realised we were lost. And not long after that the raft became stuck on a sunken log.

That was when Max started to panic.

We were well aware of the fact that the swamp was, at times, home to a few individuals who had no other place to go, and they lived in there, surviving on what they found in people's rubbish bins at night.

They were generally harmless, but could give you quite a fright when they suddenly appeared out of nowhere, all wild hair and beards, clutching bottles in paper bags.

Some years back one of them had even died in the swamp, and there were rumours that his ghost still appeared in there at times, or that just his red eyes peered through the gloom at anyone who was silly enough to stray off the more frequented paths.

Max became convinced that someone or something unpleasant was going to come and get us, and no-one would ever know what happened, as we'd been very careful not to tell our parents we were building a raft to go exploring in the swamp. Parents are always worried about things like drowning and tiger snakes and strangers, and Max suddenly started to understand why.

And I have to admit, it was scary in there, with the rain pounding down around us and our visibility cut to about three or four metres. If you weren't careful, you started to see things among the trees. Shapes of people moving, things slithering, stuff like that.

And when some large bird suddenly took off from a bunch of reeds near where we were stuck, Max lost it completely.

He let out a screech which would have got him a part in any slice-and-dice movie he wanted to audition for, and he was off the raft and thrashing through the metre-deep water bellowing at the top of his voice. It took Michael and me about three seconds before we were off after him.

We were only lost for about half and hour, I think, but to us it seemed like forever. Everything was a bit of a blur, with the trees and reeds slapping at us as we ran, the rain pounding down and Max baying like the hound of the Baskervilles. How many times we fell and felt the shallow waters close over our heads I have no idea, but it happened more than once.

Then, all of a sudden, we were out of the swamp and standing, dripping wet and coated with mud and slime, at the edge of the highway.

The other two vowed they'd never set foot in the swamp again, but I never felt quite the same way about it. Even though I'd panicked with them, there was still a part of me that got quite a thrill out of what was happening. I kind of liked the fear that overtook everything, the sense of danger and things out there that you couldn't quite see.

I wanted to go back the next day and get the raft, but the other two wouldn't have a bar of it. And there was no way I would have been able to move it without their help.

I'd tried to talk to Zac about it and he just nodded and smiled.

'You like the adrenalin rush,' he'd said.

I had to look adrenalin up in the dictionary.

Then he promised to help me build a canoe.

'It's a lot more functional that some silly old raft,' he'd told me. 'And you won't get stuck as often. All we'll need is a piece of corrugated iron without any holes in it, some tar to make a seal and a couple of pieces of wood. We could knock it up in an afternoon, maybe during your holidays.'

Zac's strength had always been a mystery to me, especially since I'm such a wimp. Even before the accident he was strong, and he liked to wear tight black T-shirts to emphasise his broad shoulders and the swell of his biceps. And when he started to use the wheelchair to exercise, his top half swelled to extraordinary proportions.

It was like he had muscles on muscles, and when he had to use his strength they'd just swell up out of him like there was something living under the skin of his arms.

We were in the shed putting together the canoe, and the sheet of corrugated iron we were using had to be bent in half. Zac just sort of grabbed it, pulled it up off the ground and balanced it on his head, then pulled down with his arms.

It folded around him as easily as paper, sitting on his head like a gigantic, bizarre hat.

'Do you think you might be able to help me get this thing off my head,' he muttered from inside his metal covering. 'I feel kind of silly sitting here like this. Mum or Dad may come in and think I've gone slightly madder than usual.'

'Sorry,' I replied, and awkwardly eased it off his head, collapsing off to one side with its weight.

'It's rather heavy,' I said. 'How will I ever get it down to the swamp? And, more importantly, will it float?'

'Oh, it'll float all right. We just have to be careful about its balance. And we'll build a little cart so you can tow it along behind your bike. Nothing to worry about. Now help me out of this chair so I can prop myself up against the bench there. I'll need to be a bit lower down to fix these lumps of wood at the front and back.'

'Fore and aft, you mean.'

'Aye aye, capt'n.'

I sort of tumbled him out of the chair and helped him to the bench, where he proceeded to grab the iron and start bending the sections into shape with his bare hands.

'Have you seen the girl next door?' I inquired, as casually as I could.

'I've seen all three of them,' he replied, concentrating on his task. 'But I presume you mean the older one, not the twins. The twins are a bit young for you.'

'I haven't met the twins, but the older one introduced herself this morning. Her name's Edith. She climbed the fence.'

'Kind of cute, lots of rings through her nose and stuff?'

'Yeah.'

'She watches us out the front window when we go running in the morning.'

'Really? I hadn't noticed.'

'Of course not.'

'No, really, I hadn't seen her until this morning.'

Zac looked up and grinned.

'I suppose not. You're always all tuckered out when we get back, hunched over your handlebars like you'd just ridden in some marathon. Your eyes all glazed, mind on breakfast.'

'Thanks a lot.'

'So what about her? She ask you out or something? Wants to get her hands on your athlete's body?'

'Very funny. She wants to go running with us.'

'Has she got wheels?'

'Nope.'

'Then she'll never keep up, will she?'

'Oh, I don't know about that. She looks pretty fit.'

He seemed to think about it for a while, twisting the iron sheet in his hands.

'Yeah, I don't see why not. She'll get totally stuffed trying to keep up and that'll be the end of it. You might have to give her a lift back on your bike. That could be fun.'

Swampland

But it wasn't the end of it at all, it was the start of everything.

It seemed so ordinary at the time, such an innocent thing, to go out running with the new neighbour, the girl next door.

But it wasn't.

And I think that, deep down, Zac knew it.

3

She more than kept up.

In fact, we had trouble keeping up with her. Or at least I did. The pace didn't seem to bother Zac that much.

The only reason Zac stayed slightly behind her was that I think he liked to watch her running; she was so fluid, made the whole thing look so easy, as if it were second nature to her.

Zac was always a little sad and distant after the runs with Edie, like he'd just been a part of something, or had witnessed a memory, that he'd never really be able to appreciate properly ever again.

More than anything, I think, she reminded him of what he used to be like, at home with his body, in control and able to do anything he put his mind to.

After the first few times we ran together, Edie and Zac began this competitive banter. They'd fire off comments at each other as we trundled through the early morning streets like some bizarre circus.

Edie would be in the lead, her legs moving without effort, long stride after long stride, as if nothing in the world could stop her, then Zac would follow, his arms turning the wheels of the chair with powerful sweeps, muscles bunching and releasing; and finally there'd be me, a soggy blob on the bike, legs turning to jelly, face red and eyes almost closed with the effort of keeping up, my clothes soaked with sweat.

I was a mess, an embarrassment, the clown of the whole performance. And if it wasn't for the fact that I felt that I had a right to be there, since it was me she had asked for permission in the first place, I think I would have given up early in the piece.

There are times when I'm so bloody-minded it amazes even myself.

It would usually start with a comment from Edie, thrown back over her shoulder while she strode out ahead of us.

'Hey, check out our chubby. He looks like he's about to burst a blood vessel or something.'

Zac would laugh as he looked back at my strained and streaming face, but I think the laugh was more for her benefit than out of real amusement.

'Oh, he'll be all right. Think of all that fat he's wearing off. In a few months he'll be able to get a part in *Speed*. He'll be a regular Keanu Reeves if he can keep this up.'

I felt I had about as much in common with Keanu Reeves as I did with Madonna, but I'd usually be too puffed to mention that at the time. The best I could do was breathe, and even that took more effort than I felt I was capable of.

How anyone can talk and exercise at the same time is beyond me.

Once they'd finished having a go at me they'd then start on each other.

'Speaking of handicaps, how do you manage to run with all that heavy metal hanging off your nose and ears?' Zac would shout out at her over the sound of the chair and my gasping breath.

'Same way you do with those wheels attached to your backside, halftrack,' she'd giggle back at him. 'Pure willpower and a dose of muscle.'

'Must give you a stiff neck holding that weight up all the time.'

'No worse than the pain in the neck you're giving me.'

And so on and so on.

Calling Zac halftrack annoyed me no end, as I didn't think anyone from outside the family had any right to be so familiar with his condition, but it never seemed to bother him. To tell the truth, he seemed to like it, as if by acknowledging his condition, she was also accepting him as a whole person.

Accepting him for what he was.

I also thought the term halftrack was insulting until I looked up the definition and found it to be quite accurate, almost complimentary.

She seemed to have a way with nicknames, although I wasn't exactly wrapped in mine. At school a couple of people I knew referred to me as 'marvellous', but I had the vague feeling they weren't being at all complimentary, especially since I was usually called that on the sports field after I'd done something unusually dumb.

'Marvellous marvellous,' they'd call, as I lay there covered in a coating of mud and shame watching our opponents score.

I'm not a sports-minded individual and don't think I ever will be, but school being what school is I have to compete with everyone else, no matter how undignified it makes me feel.

And even though I really didn't have to keep Zac company on his morning runs anymore, I continued. So I guess I was competing. But I'm not sure if I was competing against the two of them or just her. There was always this uneasy feeling inside me—or there was after the first couple of times she came out on the runs with us—that she was taking him away from me. That the closeness I had begun to achieve with my brother after he came back to himself after the accident was about to go away.

There was no way I was going to let that happen, or so I thought.

I guess I was wrong about that as well.

On the other hand, there's the fact that I may have been concerned about Zac taking Edie away from me. I'd been the first one to meet her, after all; had brought her along on the runs and everything.

The sight of her pounding away on the footpath a couple of metres in front of me was enough, in itself, to keep me struggling away at the pedals every morning, oblivious to the fact that I was in more physical pain than I'd ever experienced in my life.

Who knows what makes anyone do anything?

✸✸✸✸✸✸✸

The twins were a completely different kettle of fish from Edie, and I use that phrase intentionally.

They were exceptionally ugly.

They looked like fish.

Particularly nasty fish with big, popping eyes.

The kind you wouldn't want to run into late one night in a dark aquarium.

I suppose they were around ten years old, but even that was difficult to tell.

They had strange, fat faces and protuberant lips, and when they smiled they exposed a row (a row each, to be more accurate, but for some reason you always talked about them like they were one person) of odd, peg-like teeth.

The teeth themselves had a blue pallor, as if their owners had been eating berries or something.

Their hair was white, brilliantly so, as if it had been dyed, though Edie told me it was their natural colour, and they wore it slicked back over their skulls like a helmet. When you combined this with the fact that they had very large heads on top of broad shoulders, with the rest of their bodies tapering away to tiny, doll-like feet, it gave the impression of cartoon characters travelling at great speed.

Which was something they did, getting everywhere at an incredible rate of knots, chattering to each other in their whispering voices.

You could be standing in the backyard of our house working on something and you'd hear them on the other side of the fence, and the next second—or so it seemed—they'd be there at your elbow grinning up at you.

They were absolutely identical, even in the way they dressed.

Edie said their names were Violet and Mauve, but she always referred to them as Yin and Yang.

'It's because they sleep in the same bed,' she told me one day after I'd asked repeatedly after the source of the nicknames, 'head to toe like they're encased in some sort of pod. They've always been like that, ever since they were born. They both have their own beds, but you'll always find them in one or the other. Nothing my parents do has ever been able to change that, apart from putting them in separate rooms and locking the door, which is more like locking them up in prison than putting them to bed. When they tried that the twins were up all night crying their eyes out, so Mum and Dad just gave up. They reckon they'll grow out of it some day, but I'm not so sure. You never see them apart. They even take baths and go to the toilet at the same time.'

I found that really strange, and had this bizarre image of the two of them sharing a toilet bowl, one on each side, as if they were joined down the middle of their backs.

Zac took to calling them Hellspawn and Hemlock, but never in Edie's presence.

'They're creepy,' he said to me one day. 'I always see them coming out of the swamp, all huddled over together, whispering away like they've got some sort of secret. Every time they see me they start giggling and slink off inside the house. I don't like being alone with them. It makes my skin crawl they're so ugly. Which is weird, because Edie's not too hard on the eyes, don't you reckon?'

I had to agree with him.

When the police arrived at our door early one Saturday morning I was not totally surprised, though it had been some time since they'd paid us a visit. My first thought was that something had finally happened to Mum's sister, Aunt Lisa, down in Melbourne, as we'd had a few family panics about her health in the past, but that wasn't the case.

I'd got quite used to the police during the time Zac was running wild, stealing things and getting into fights, but they'd been scarce ever since the accident. The only figure of authority to appear on a regular basis was his parole officer, and her visits were now so far apart they were scarcely worth worrying about. Zac only had another month or so of that to go.

But, for once, it wasn't Zac they wanted to see, it was me.

Dad, complete with worried brow, brought them into the kitchen where I was scoffing down slice after slice of Vegemite toast (another result of the increased morning exercise was that I now ate twice as much as I did before, but the good thing about it was that I didn't seem to put on any more weight). Zac was at the table as well, and the moment he saw the uniforms his whole body went rigid, which is easy to understand.

There were two of them, a woman constable who couldn't have been much older than Zac and a huge red-faced bloke who seemed to fill the kitchen and made our father, who's a bit more than average in size, look like a child.

'Hello Zac,' the man said. He seemed friendly enough and when he smiled it looked like he meant it.

'Officer Donleavy,' Zac replied, wheeling his chair out from the table and taking a position directly in front of the two police officers. 'What can I help you with this morning?'

Zac wasn't being anywhere near as friendly as the police.

Donleavy grinned and shook his head.

'You can't help us with anything, Zac. I'm here to see your brother.'

From behind I heard my mother gasp.

'It's all right, dear,' my father said, coming around the table and putting his arm around her, 'they've told me what it's all about. Marvin hasn't done anything wrong, they just want to ask some questions. He might be able to help them, that's all.'

'What do you reckon he's done?' asked Zac, belligerently.

'Like your father just said, Zac, nothing. We're asking questions of all the young boys around here. Ask anyone. We've been working our way down the street.'

'It's all right, Zac,' Dad said. 'Let the officers sit down. They might like a cup of tea or something.'

Zac made a loud snorting noise through his nose and wheeled himself back to the table.

The woman smiled at me and introduced herself.

'Hi Marvin, I'm Constable Vacchs.'

I mumbled hello and looked intently at the crumbs on the table. I hadn't done anything wrong, I knew that, but it didn't stop me feeling guilty all the same.

'You don't have to be frightened, Marvin, we only want to ask some questions,' she continued.

'I'm not frightened,' I said, my voice making me sound just the opposite.

Zac and Donleavy sat gulping tea and staring at each other, oblivious to everyone else at the table.

'I suppose you've heard about all the pets that have been disappearing around here?' she asked.

'You mean Blitz?'

'Blitz?' She looked puzzled.

'Old Marty's dog,' Donleavy said without taking his eyes off Zac. 'The bloke that lives down at the edge of the swamp.'

'Oh, that's right. Sorry, I didn't remember the dog's name. Yes, Marvin, like that. What have you heard?'

'Nothing,' I replied, which was the truth.

'What about any others?' she kept on.

'I haven't heard about any others.'

'What's this leading to, officer?' my mother asked, a definite quaver in her voice. My mother was always nervous about the police, which was understandable, since every time they'd visited us before it was usually to drag Zac off for something or other.

'Rather a lot of pets have gone missing from around here over the last two weeks, Mrs Thomas,' she said.

'Fourteen in two weeks, to be exact,' continued Donleavy. 'One a day. We've even found a couple of them, and what happened to Blitz was pleasant by comparison.'

'That's disgusting,' my father added. 'Neither of my children would have anything to do with something like that.'

Donleavy let out a long sigh.

'I keep trying to tell all of you, we're not suggesting that either Marvin or Zac had anything to do with it. We're just asking if they've either seen or heard something that might help us. Just because Zac's had a run-in or two with us before doesn't mean we, and especially *I*, think that anyone in this family would do anything sick to an animal.'

He looked directly at Zac.

'You may have had a wild streak, Zac, but you never did anything cruel. We're pretty sure it's kids who are doing this and we just want to know if Marvin's heard anything.'

'He hasn't,' said Zac. 'Have you, Marvin?'

I shook my head and continued to stare at the table crumbs.

'Well, fine,' Vacchs said, getting up from the table. 'Thanks for the tea, Mrs Fisher, sorry we bothered you. You will let us know if you hear anything, won't you Marvin?'

'Don't worry, he will,' said my father as he followed them out of the kitchen.

Donleavy stopped in the doorway and looked back at Zac.

'I hear you're training for the Paralympics.'

'Might be,' Zac muttered.

'Well I'm glad to know you're doing something. Making the best of things, you know? From the look of your arms you'll probably win, too.'

'Thanks.'

'Just don't let me catch you speeding.'

They stared at each other for a minute, then Donleavy winked and Zac burst out laughing.

He was still laughing when I heard the front door close behind the departing officers.

That was the first any of us heard about the pets, apart from old Blitz, who we'd known about since the day he disappeared. But once we did know, it seemed to be the only thing that people in the neighbourhood talked about, probably because the police had been going around that Saturday asking everyone. Even my mate Michael had had the family cat disappear, but no sign of it ever turned up like some of the others had. No-one's parents really wanted to talk about what had been done to the animals that had been found, and that was enough to get everyone speculating in the most gruesome of manners. There were all sorts of rumours floating about, mostly to do with black magic and sacrifices, but none of us really knew the truth of the matter. Those with more rational minds were saying that it was one of the homeless people that you occasionally saw in the swamp, but the police had been right through the place and it didn't appear that anyone was living in there at the time. Max was all in favour of some slime creature that only came up from below the waters at night and fed on little animals that strayed into its path, which was another reason to stay the hell away from the place. But that was just Max being

Max, and I knew he was scared of the place because of the raft incident and invented things to make his fear more understandable to himself. As for myself, I didn't have any thoughts on the matter at all. The idea of doing something cruel or violent to anything, let alone a helpless animal, was so alien to me that I couldn't even speculate on the matter. Though I reckon Zac had an idea, but he wasn't sharing it with anyone.

4

True to his word, Zac helped me finish the canoe, and even though it had been made from bits of scrap metal and wood it was a thing of real beauty, even if I do say so myself.

We'd finished it—or so I thought—late one afternoon.

After he'd got the metal bent into the shape he wanted, Zac fastened pieces of wood fore and aft with nails and then sealed it completely with melted tar. Once this had dried he got me to jump around inside it, so that the base of it flattened out and the sides spread. Another piece of wood was then jammed down in the middle and sealed in place with more nails and tar. This gave it the appearance of one of those Native American canoes from the old Westerns that Dad liked to watch on the television. It was higher and pointed at either end where the metal was sealed to the wood and spread quite broad in the middle where my jumping had flattened out the bottom. Another section of wood was holding the sides apart.

I went to bed satisfied that I had a functional, if inelegant, water vehicle.

But it was a lot more than that in the morning.

That night, Zac talked Dad into helping him, after

first convincing him that nothing untoward could happen to me in a swamp where the water was no more than a metre deep. He also promised Dad that he'd give me a long lecture about water safety, snakes, talking to strangers and a million other things that he briefly mentioned to me in passing.

Dad had also said he'd talk to Mum so that she wouldn't throw a fit when she saw me peddling away towards the swamp with a canoe sticking out the back of my bike.

Overnight, my canoe had been turned into a work of art.

The outside was brilliant gloss red with two large purple and black eyes painted at the front over a snarling mouth full of shark teeth. Inside it was bright yellow and he'd fashioned two small black seats, one on either side of the wood brace, which you could sit on while paddling.

He'd also made two single-bladed paddles, one of which was red, the other yellow.

In beautiful script lettering on the other end of the canoe from the eyes and mouth he'd painted the words, *SWAMP THING*.

I was speechless, which Zac said was thanks enough as far as he was concerned.

We spent half the day slapping together a small trolley-like structure to carry it on, demolishing an old billy cart I hadn't used in years. As long as I didn't try any fast manoeuvres or sharp turns, I could quite easily carry it behind my bike.

Which I wanted to do immediately.

'Don't drown, okay?' Zac said to me, grinning at my enthusiasm. 'You'll make me look like a right twit after what I promised Dad.'

'Can't you come?' I asked. 'Maybe just part-way?'

'No, mate,' he said, looking a little sad at the invitation. 'You know this thing can't go off road.' He laughed. 'Remember the last time I tried that, just after I started running in the mornings and took that short cut across the spare block over near the Brin's place? It was an hour before anyone found me. I got bogged right up to the axle.' He made shooing motions with his hands.

'Don't you worry about me, just concentrate on staying afloat. These things aren't as easy to manage as they make it look in the movies.'

⁂

The first thing I did was get totally soaked through.

I'd managed to pedal down to the edge of the swamp that was closest to the waterways without any trouble, the trolley and canoe bouncing along behind the bike like they were born to be there.

Along the way I was singing out loud, I was so happy—one of the songs my Mum used to play on the old turntable when she didn't think anyone was home . . . *born to be wiiild . . . nyaaah, nyaaah, nyah nyah, nyaaah, nyaaah, nyah nyah . . .* or something like that anyway. It seemed the right choice of words for the occasion.

Anyway, after pedalling the bike into the swamp as far as I could manage, I unhooked the canoe and dragged it along behind me all the way to the water's edge. It was surprisingly easy to carry around on the trolley, and I didn't have anywhere near as much trouble as I'd been anticipating.

That was to come later.

I stuck one end of the trolley in the water, pulled the rubber straps off, and the canoe slid straight down into the murky green water. I'd attached a piece of rope to the aft end and already had that tied to a tree branch so it didn't float away.

It looked so perfect, I sat on the bank for a while just looking at it bobbing gently and swinging out from the bank with the gentle breeze that was blowing. The brilliant red and yellow colours were such a vibrant contrast to the usual drab grey-green of the swamp I kept trying to find an image to represent it . . . a flower blooming in a rubbish dump or something like that.

And when I felt the moment was exactly right, I pulled the canoe in close and stepped carefully into the middle.

It immediately slid out from under my feet and up-ended me full length into the water.

I was in such a hurry to get to the surface I came up underneath the canoe and banged my head so hard I saw stars *and* stripes.

Spluttering water and cursing my stupid self-confidence, I dragged myself to shore. The canoe sat bobbing on the water as if it was laughing at me, and I vowed that the next time my brother warned me to be careful about something I'd listen to him—really, really listen to him.

Which, of course, I never did.

After a bit of experimenting with my balance I finally got the canoe under control and was able to get it to go in the direction I wanted. I learned to handle the paddle without too much trouble and found that by kneeling with my bum on the seat and legs either side I could keep the canoe very steady.

A couple of dips of the paddle and I was surging ahead with confidence, moving down the avenues between the paperbarks like it was second nature to me.

Swampland

I felt like I was far away from the neighbourhood, in the swamps of Louisiana or something, with 'gators lurking in the reeds along the bank and strange swamp folk peering out of the foliage at me.

There was the sound of birds and frogs to keep me company and the lapping of the water against the sides of the canoe. Every now and then something larger rustled off through the undergrowth as I passed and the sensation of being cut off from everything civilised, everything I was used to and comfortable with, increased every time I dipped the paddle.

At any second I expected to hear the sound of a banjo playing in the distance or the murmur of Cajun voices.

I had been passing along a long, thin body of water in a place where the trees almost grew across and blocked out the sunlight when all of a sudden the foliage gave way and I emerged into a large, open area that was like a small lake.

Slipping the paddle into the bottom of the canoe I let myself simply drift out into the open expanse of water. It wasn't gigantic or anything, about the size of a few blocks of land, but having come out of the small channel which was all overgrown it felt like I'd just emerged into Lake Victoria.

'I name thee Lake Marvellous, in honour of myself,' I called out loudly, liking the thought of being the first person to have sailed on these waters.

It was really quite beautiful. The paperbarks all crowded closely on the banks, and where there weren't trees the reeds were very high and dense, so it was like being inside a sort of auditorium. Great clouds of dragonflies swarmed across the water, dipping down occasionally and touching the surface, causing sudden sparkles of light as the tiny ripples moved out and away.

There was a slight insect hum in the air and whenever a breeze blew there was a soft, sighing sound as if the area itself was breathing.

I'd probably floated to the middle of the lake when I noticed something at the other side, sort of half-submerged in the water. There was something unnatural about it, a sense of being man-made and familiar, but it was difficult to tell, so I picked up my paddle and headed towards it.

The closer I got the more familiar it became.

When I was a couple of metres away I realised why. What was lying there was the raft that we'd made those couple of months before, the one we'd discarded in such a confused hurry the day the rain came down and panic set in.

And though we'd been unsure of where we were at the time, unable to really see clearly and with our imaginations working overtime, I was pretty sure this wasn't where we'd abandoned it, though it was impossible to be certain of that. All I could really remember was leaping off the boat after Max, falling headfirst into the water and what seemed like hours of running around in the rain bumping into trees and tripping over into the mud.

We'd probably run around in circles for most of the time, as people tend to do when they're frightened.

However, from what I could remember, we weren't in any open area of water, but as we couldn't see we really wouldn't have known where we were. And anyway, the raft could easily have been floating around in here for weeks before it found its way onto Lake Marvellous and settled in the mud and reeds in this particular dark corner.

But that didn't account for the fact that someone had obviously been using it, though not for the task it was originally intended.

The raft was firmly wedged against the bank and from the look of it someone had gone to some effort to make sure it never moved again. Holes had been punched into the sides of the 44 gallon drums, lots of them, as if someone had been at it with an axe. And the reeds all around the raft had been pulled across and woven together, so the raft appeared like it was inside a small cavern or that it was being used as the floor of a primitive cubby. All over the platform of the raft were the stubs of a wide variety of candles, from tiny ones you'd see on a birthday cake through to the gigantic type you find in those not-so-trendy hippy shops that sell incense and crystals and things.

When you were close to the raft you could smell the perfume of the candles mixed with something else, something dark and sticky and nasty.

I pulled the canoe right up to its edge and had a good look at it, peering into the gloom that was created by the woven roof of reeds. You couldn't quite see all the raft. It disappeared into darkness, but you could really smell it.

It was very unpleasant, a combination of incense, burnt candle wax and roadkill.

This little corner of the lake felt completely different from the rest of it, silent and strange, in contrast to the sparkling dragonfly water behind me.

And cold. Really cold like I'd just drifted into a freezer.

The platform itself seemed to be covered in something dark, and when I put my hand out to touch it it came away sticky.

Things happened very quickly then.

I lifted my hand up to my nose to sniff whatever it was that had come away on my fingers and happened to glance right back into the darkness of the reed cavern.

There were eyes there.

At first I thought it was just two pinpricks of light coming through the reeds, but then they blinked and I froze where I was, hand up to my nose, staring at those nasty little points of light that were directed at me.

I was holding my breath, unsure of what was going to happen and not certain at all of what I was looking at, or what was looking at me. The story of the homeless man who had died somewhere in the swamp suddenly didn't seem as silly anymore.

Then the canoe and I simply took off.

Backwards.

And I fell face down into the canoe, letting out a shriek of surprise that must have scared the hell out of all the nearby wildlife, because by the time I'd got myself upright again the air was full of flapping wings and startled, squawking birds.

Not that I was spending a lot of time looking at them, because the canoe was still moving backwards across the lake at such speed that it was creating large waves on either side.

I wasn't shrieking anymore, being too busy hanging onto the sides of the canoe, but I was making a pathetic 'unh, unh, unh' noise in the back of my throat as I looked over my shoulder to see what was dragging me along. What I wanted at that moment—all I wanted in the world—was not to fall out of the canoe. Whatever it was that propelled me across the lake appeared to be under the water, and if it was under the water I wanted to make sure that I was on top.

Even better, I wanted to be on dry land, but I certainly wasn't going to chance swimming it.

And then, just as the canoe reached the opposite end of the lake, whatever was dragging it let go.

I coasted along for a brief period of time and then just sat there bobbing and rocking slightly, the only sound now being the wash of the bow waves as they slapped against the bank.

It took me some time to move, as I didn't want to let go of the sides in case we suddenly started moving again. But when a great bubble of air broke the surface of the water in the middle of the lake I had the paddle back in my hands and was moving along the overgrown channel as fast as I could manage without up-ending myself.

My heart was pounding in my chest like it wanted to get out, much as I wanted to get out of the swamp, and my arms were working overtime, the paddle pushing the canoe through the water like a knife.

I didn't know what had happened and I wasn't going to stay to find out. All I wanted was dry land, my bike and a good, solid road underneath me.

Enough of this seafaring adventure crap, I thought.

But by the time I reached the place I'd launched from earlier in the day it was like I'd been through a bad dream or some sort of hallucination. Everything was as it should be. There was the trolley and my bike, the sun was shining and you could hear frogs and birds as if nothing had happened.

I jumped out onto the bank, backed away from the water and looked back along the way I'd come.

Nothing was following me. The only ripples in the water were from the canoe.

I contemplated leaving it where it was, but when I thought about what I'd say to Zac I changed my mind.

What would I say?

'Hi Zac. Sorry about the canoe. I saw some horrid little eyes and something grabbed it and dragged me across a lake. Thought I'd just leave it behind and maybe go back in a couple of years to get it. Maybe after the swamp's been drained.'

It sounded pathetic, even to me.

Very carefully, my eyes never leaving the water in case I saw some dangerous-looking ripples, I pulled the canoe out and put it back on the trolley.

As I rode away I thought I heard soft, whispering laughter, but it seemed to come from a long way off and I was pretty sure it was my imagination playing tricks on me.

At least I hoped it was my imagination.

Nothing can laugh under water, after all.

5

'What sort of things live in swamps?' I asked Edie a couple of days later.

We were sitting out the back of my house late in the afternoon, having spent the day in town going through the local museum.

I'm not normally a museum type, but since the episode in the swamp I'd developed something of an interest in local wildlife, especially anything that lived under water. The museum seemed the right sort of place to start, especially since everything in there was dead as well as stuffed.

Nothing dangerous there, I'd reasoned; lots of thick glass between me and the exhibits as well.

I had an overwhelming desire to feel safe.

Since Edie had been hanging around a bit, wanting to go out to the movies and things like that, I'd asked her if she felt like coming along. She'd agreed readily enough, but once we were there she hadn't shown much interest in anything, wandering from exhibit to exhibit with a glazed look in her eyes.

'Nothing moves,' I'd heard her mutter to herself. 'Not a damn thing moving anywhere.'

I'd offered to buy her lunch but she even turned that down.

'Not a lot there takes my fancy,' she said, running her eyes across the spread of ready-made sandwiches and smiling her little pointy-toothed smile.

I never realised how big the museum actually was and we called it quits after about four hours, having only seen half of what there was on show. To my great regret, we hadn't even come close to the wetlands display, which had been my original intention. Not wanting to divulge my obsession to Edie, however, I hadn't headed straight for it, thinking we'd get there eventually, but I'd misjudged the size of the place. And by the time we were in the general vicinity Edie had had enough and we'd caught the bus home.

Hence my question.

'Why do you want to know about swamps?' she asked, reasonably enough.

'I don't know. Just interested. Like to know what's there when I go canoeing, that's all.'

'You go canoeing in the swamp?' Her voice rose slightly when she said this, and she looked at me strangely, almost as if I'd just done something incredibly stupid.

'Yeah, of course I do. Where else do you think I'd go with a canoe?'

'I didn't even know you had a canoe!'

'It's in the shed. Zac made it for me last week.'

'Snakes,' she said. 'Lots and lots of snakes.'

'I know about snakes. And they're not going to worry anyone in a canoe.'

'What about water snakes?'

'Do we have them here?'

'Yeah,' she continued, sounding quite pleased with herself, 'and there's eels, too. Giant eels. And . . . and snapping turtles!'

'Giant eels? Snapping turtles? Give me a break.'

'It's true.'

'Rubbish!'

'I've got a book on it. You stay right there.'

She was over the fence in seconds. I sat there staring ahead of me.

'Giant eels,' I muttered. 'No such thing in this country. She's been reading too much Jules Verne or something. I've never heard of a snapping turtle.'

It didn't take long before she was back in the chair next to me holding a rather large encyclopedia-looking book entitled *Freshwater Giants*. The book appeared to be quite a few years old and had seen a lot of use.

Edie flipped through the pages like she knew what she was doing.

'Ahhhh, here we go,' she said, flipping the book open to show me a photograph of a line of grim-looking men holding the most gigantic eel I had ever seen in my life. It had a head on it that would have looked more at home on a bull and a mouth full of extremely evil teeth.

The really scary thing was that it took five men to hold it.

'Now that,' said Edie with evident satisfaction, 'is what I call an eel. They live in fresh water too, not that you'd call the swamp all that fresh.'

I think my mouth must have been hanging open because right at that second a fly managed to get caught in my throat and I ended up on the ground coughing and spluttering and making nasty little hoicking noises. Tears were pouring from my eyes.

Edie got down on the ground to help me, and after a vigorous pummelling on the back that felt like it was done by an international rugby player, I managed to cough the horrid little thing up. It landed on the book we'd been reading and as I guiltily reached over to wipe it away Edie's hand shot out and picked it off.

'Hey, don't worry about it,' she said, smiling across at me. 'Are you okay? You gave me quite a fright there. I thought my eel picture had given you an asthma attack or something.'

I nodded and she brushed her fingers across her lips and then pushed the hair back behind her ear. It was a very casual movement, easy and unaffected, and I realised for the first time just how beautiful she was.

She gave me this funny look from under her eyelashes, as if she knew exactly what I was thinking, smiled to herself and rose gracefully from the ground.

I got up with her, wondering briefly where she had put the dead fly, and picked up the book.

'So what's this snapping turtle thing?' I croaked.

'Page seventy-five, third paragraph down,' she replied, without even seeming to think.

We must have spent over an hour going through that book before it was time for her to go home. We looked at pictures and read descriptions of a whole range of disgustingly huge things that lived in fresh water all around the world, from three-metre-long catfish through to turtles that can bite off fingers and toes and had been known to take small children. The swamp had never appeared less inviting. Though I must admit, not a lot of these creatures lived in Australia, except for the Murray Cod, and we didn't live anywhere near that river.

But the thing was, I don't think I registered any of it, not really.

I was feeling quite strange and was having a lot of trouble keeping my eyes on what we were reading. All I wanted to do was look at Edie's neck, the colour of her skin just along the edge of her hairline, the way I could see the sinews moving when she turned to look at something or nodded her head. Even the earrings and studs that were shoved through her skin started to look attractive to me, and I wondered what it would be like to have an ear pierced or maybe a stud put in my nose.

All the while Edie kept taking me through the book, glancing across at me occasionally, always with that small, sly smile on her lips.

'You can keep the book for a day or so,' she said eventually, 'but I've got to have it back. It was my dad's, and it's about the only thing of his I have.'

She reached over and stroked the side of my face and smiled. Then she was over the fence and gone, leaving me staring after her.

I reached over and put my hand on the seat she'd just vacated and could just feel a slight warmth from where she'd been sitting. I sat there with my hand on the chair until the sun was gone completely and I was stiff from sitting still for so long.

When I finally came inside Zac was sitting at the window near the back door with a questioning look on his face, but when I went to say something to him he just turned his chair around and squeaked off towards his room.

It wasn't until much later that night that what she'd said just before leaving registered with me.

I was sitting up in bed, idly flicking through Edie's book, trying to find anything that could have—even by accident—ended up in our swamp, when I happened to notice the name written on the page inside the front jacket.

It was written in a strong, certain hand, the letters of the name almost cutting through the page itself: Dr Randolph Fischer.

Nothing about Tucker anywhere.

All thoughts of giant eels left my mind and I was suddenly very curious about Edie's origins.

If Mr and Mrs Tucker weren't her real parents, who was? Maybe Mrs Tucker had remarried? It certainly wasn't uncommon, even in our neighbourhood. At least half of everyone I knew had either divorced or separated parents. Some only knew their mothers and had never even seen their fathers, so it wasn't a new concept to me.

The thing was, though, everyone I knew talked quite openly about it.

You know the sort of thing . . . 'Hi, I'm Sylvia, I'm fourteen years old and my parents are divorced.'

There were even times when I felt quite left out because my parents were still together.

And then it occurred to me that I didn't even know where the Tucker family had come from. They just arrived that day in the middle of the fog, almost like they'd come out of nowhere, and not one of them had said a thing about where they'd been before.

I resolved to have a few questions answered the next day.

When I finally drifted off to sleep my dreams were populated by things I couldn't quite see, things that swam and dived through my mind armed with razor-sharp teeth and hooked beaks that tore at my fingers and toes.

⁂

She was adopted. So were the twins.

The funny thing was, the moment I asked she came

right out with it, almost as if she had been waiting for me to ask, as if she'd supplied all the clues and I had just been a little slow in getting them.

'Our parents were scientists,' she told me, her eyes downcast while she spoke. 'They died in an accident years ago, just after the twins were born. I hardly remember them, and Mauve and Violet have no recollection of them at all. But the Tuckers knew them really well. They were all friends at university, so we've got lots of pictures and everything, when they were younger.'

She continued to stare at the ground.

'So how come you ended up with the Tuckers?' I asked.

'They can't have kids. My real parents had asked them to look after us if anything ever happened to them—had it all written up legally and everything—so it just sort of fell into place like that. The Tuckers have been really good, though. I think of them as our real parents now.'

'What about the twins?'

'I don't know, really. They're not close to anyone, except maybe me. It's like they live in a world of their own.'

'Where were you from? Originally, I mean.'

'New Zealand. But we were living in America when the accident happened. The Tuckers flew over and brought us back to Auckland. That's one of my first real memories, the plane flight. I can remember crying, wanting my Mum and Dad, and the twins were screaming all the time and throwing up over everything. There was a hostess on the plane who kept trying to get me interested in drawing and stuff, but I just wanted to go home.'

'So that's why you say fush instead of fish.'

She looked up at me and grinned.

'And I thought you were unobservant.'

'Not me. I'm just a bit chubby.'

That made her laugh out loud, and for some reason it made me feel inexpressibly happy, like I'd just won a grand prize in a lottery.

'So your name's really Edith Fischer?'

'No. It's Tucker. It was changed when we were legally adopted.'

'It's a nice name, either way.'

She reached over, took my hand and smiled.

That's when I really fell for her. Hook, line and sinker.

During this period, even though I was attempting to find a cause for what happened to me in the swamp, the incident itself became more and more remote.

It was almost as if I'd imagined it, or that somehow what I thought had happened was not the truth at all. I began to think that perhaps I'd been caught in a gust of wind or that there'd been some sort of current moving across the lake that had swept the canoe along with it.

Whatever it was, it no longer had the level of terror for me that it had to begin with.

And since Zac had started to ask me why I wasn't using the splendid canoe he'd made—and I'd run out of excuses—I resolved to have another trip into the swamp. Maybe not onto Lake Marvellous, but certainly a cruise through some of the smaller and less threatening waterways.

Part of my confidence had also been restored through Edie's book, because even though there were some fairly horrific things that lived in swamps and rivers, none of them lived in Australian waters. And I was fairly certain that no-one in their right mind would go around introducing something as unlovely as a snapping turtle into a country where the most dangerous freshwater creature was probably a stray plastic bag.

6

It was a glorious day, all sunshine and gentle breezes filled with clouds of butterflies. I played dumb when Zac wheeled himself into my room and tried to rouse me for the morning run, muttering and mumbling into my pillow like I was deep in sleep and had no intention of waking up for something as vigorous as running. He whispered something about 'lazy good-for-nothing' and I could almost imagine the sneer on his face as he left. I lay there grinning to myself and listening to him outside my window telling Edie that 'the chubby one is out to it and not likely to stir for some hours yet'.

When I heard them take off down the driveway I leapt out of bed, already dressed in my jeans and T-shirt, pulled on my sneakers and hustled off to the shed.

The canoe was still on its trolley, so all I had to do was attach it to the back of my bike and ride, which I did, feeling the day rush into my lungs as I breathed. It was like being filled with invisible energy.

I felt wonderful, all thought of my previous experience in the swamp overwhelmed by the excitement of being up this early with nothing but my own company and the thrill of the canoe to look forward to. The clouds of butterflies swirled and parted around my head like multi-coloured curtains.

As I passed the last house in the street and left the road for the swamp I saw old Marty standing at the corner of his house in the shadow of the porch, so I waved and shouted good morning to him. He raised his hand a little as I rode by, then slunk away around the corner.

Marty had never really been the same since they found Blitz, and I really couldn't blame him. It wasn't a nice thing to do to anything, even a ratty old dog. But even that thought didn't dampen my spirits any.

I followed the path down to where it met the water and unloaded the canoe.

That morning in the swamp was one of the best I'd ever had, though I made a point of studiously avoiding Lake Marvellous. It wasn't that I felt worried about the place all that much, having now convinced myself that it was more an aberration of nature combined with my rather over-fertile imagination that had been the cause of it, but just to be on the safe side I simply didn't head in its direction.

It was a reasonable-sized swamp, after all, and there was a lot of it that was under water.

There's a lot of life in a swamp if you know what to look for and you're quiet about looking. Apart from the rather obvious things like birds and insects and frogs, there are a lot of creatures that are shy of contact with humans, which is understandable when you think of what we do to them, and it takes a certain amount of stealth to get close enough to see them.

Once, when I was just floating along and holding the paddle inside the canoe, I saw a couple of long-necked tortoises sunning themselves on a half-sunken log. These are rather cute little things, only a few centimetres long, with necks almost the same length as their shells. Naturally, the first things I thought about were snapping turtles, but the comparison is ridiculous. The latter can grow to nearly a metre in length, can weigh almost 40 kilos and have huge beaks, almost as if they have the head of a giant parrot grafted onto a turtle's body. They're also native to America, so I knew I had nothing to worry about.

(A week before I wouldn't have known details like that, but it's amazing what you can learn about the world in a few nights of reading.)

I also saw a couple of water snakes, which I took pains to avoid, and quite a few cats which obviously weren't anyone's pets.

Further into the swamp, in places where I was sure I was the only one to have travelled, there were some amazing water birds that looked like things out of African nature documentaries, with long spindly legs and beaks that were thin and curved like old-fashioned daggers. They stalked through the shallow waters, and one time I saw one stab its head down and come up with a large frog wriggling on the end of it. The bird flicked its head back and tossed the frog into the air, catching it in its wide-open beak as it came down.

I vowed that the next time I came I was going to bring my camera. Maybe I could become a nature photographer, I reasoned. Zac wasn't the only one who could want to be famous.

Then, like a prize idiot, I got careless.

To begin with, I thought I'd found another lake, because I didn't enter it from the same spot as I had the first time.

Instead, I came into it at the opposite end, almost from next to where the raft had been hidden.

I had been following a very thin channel through high reeds when I came to a spot where an old paperbark had fallen and almost blocked the way. It was a toss-up between going on and turning back, but I realised that when I was almost lying down in the canoe I could see water past the blockage, and if I hunkered down and pulled the reeds as I went along I would probably make it through.

A couple of times I got stuck quite badly and thought I'd have to get out of the canoe and push, which was not a task I really relished, but eventually it came free and by the time I sat up I was drifting through open water.

There's something really pleasant about coming out of a confined space into an open area, a feeling of freedom, of release, and I just sat there for a minute enjoying it, not really looking around. I think I might even have been whistling a tune I'd heard on the radio a few days before.

Then I was struck with a strong sensation of deja vu and I knew exactly where I was. And even though the last time I had seen this same view I had been looking back over my shoulder while travelling at a rate of knots going 'unh, unh, unh' at the top of my voice, I could recognise it.

And right at that second I heard a whispering from behind me, followed by something slithering into the water.

It was an incredibly creepy noise, that slithering, like something large and scaly that was capable of moving quickly from one environment into another.

The hairs on the back of my neck immediately stood to attention and my heart started to beat at about twice its normal rate.

I looked around and saw the raft, but this time I knew there had been something there because I could see that the candle stubs were still smoking. In fact, the whole area where the raft was hidden seemed to be dense with wafting white smoke. It was oozing out between the reeds in whispery tendrils that disappeared as soon as they struck the sunlight. There also seemed to be something lying on the raft, but it was difficult to tell because of the haze. Around the raft was a thick, white substance that looked something like soap foam or sago.

But the thing that really scared me, scared me so much I felt my bowels turn uneasily the second I saw it, was the spread of ripples coming from the front of the raft. Ripples that suggested something large had just submerged itself in the water.

Without taking my eyes off the ripples, I picked up the paddle and dipped it gently in the water.

Nothing happened.

I started the canoe slowly forward.

The overgrown channel I'd entered by the first time seemed to be an eternity away.

I risked another dip of the paddle and propelled the canoe a little faster.

I realised I'd been holding my breath, so I let it out with a large whoosh and started to paddle with a lot more energy.

Then something bumped against the canoe with such force I thought I was going to fall out the other side, and in my panic to stay balanced I dropped the paddle. It floated about a metre away from me but there was nothing on earth (or off it) that was going to get me to reach for it.

I carefully lifted the spare paddle and held it above my head with one hand, the other gripping the side of the canoe so hard I could see my knuckles pure white against the red and yellow paint. As far as I was concerned, the first thing that I saw moving was going to end up with the indentation of a paddle right down the centre of its head.

But the only thing that moved was the floating paddle, which suddenly disappeared under the surface as if it had forgotten all laws of buoyancy.

I think I yelped and broke wind loudly at the same time, but I never lost my grip on either the canoe or the surviving paddle. I was beginning to feel they were the only things that were going to keep me alive.

Then I started going around in circles.

It began slowly, and for a while I thought it was just a current or the wind moving the canoe, then I realised it was being pushed from both ends in an anti-clockwise direction. It began to move faster and faster and I was forced to drop the paddle and grip the sides to stop myself tumbling out.

I could see the sides of Lake Marvellous swirling past at an ever-increasing rate, round and round, the trees and reeds blurring into a long strip of brown and green, the speed of it whipping the hair around my head and into my eyes until the tears began to flow and I was half-blinded by everything that was happening.

A constant moan was escaping from my throat and I was so dizzy that I could neither think nor see straight. It was like being caught in a tiny whirlpool of incredible force and I was helpless to do anything.

I'm not sure when I became aware of the sound, but it had definitely been there for some time before my brain was able to separate it from everything else that was happening. It was like a high-pitched screech, intense and ululating, like nothing I had ever heard before.

At the same time I also realised that whatever had been turning the canoe was gone, though it took some time before the momentum allowed it to slow to almost stopping. I was hunched over by this time with the effort of staying inside it, my hands still gripping the sides so tightly I had actually buckled the corrugated iron.

Taking a series of deep breaths to try and stop the hideous swirling in my head, I looked over the side of the canoe, and though my vision was still extremely blurred I made out two heads bobbing up out of the water. They were facing away from me and only visible for that brief second, but I knew exactly what they were.

It was the twins, Violet and Mauve.

Then they sank back under the water.

The second they disappeared the strange cry stopped as well.

Which was when I vomited, long and loud and completely. It felt like I was emptying my stomach of everything that I'd ever eaten since the time I started consuming solids.

How long I lay in the bottom of the canoe trying to get my breath and senses back to normal I have no idea, but when I finally lifted my head up and looked over the side a huge cloud of tadpoles had done a great job of removing virtually all trace of my vomiting.

The sun was directly above me.

Once again I could hear birds and frogs and the water was dead still.

I stole a quick glance at the raft and it was still there, but there was no trace of smoke or whatever had been lying on it the last time I looked. That strange foam-like substance was still around it but I had no interest in finding out what it was.

Next to the canoe was the missing paddle, but the blade looked like it had been shoved down an insinkerator. It was now only about half its normal length and one end was splintered to the point where it was unusable.

I reached over and pulled it into the canoe for a closer look. All around the splintering were what looked like teeth marks, and further up on the handle were deep, ugly scratches as if something with claws had been gripping it tightly.

The image of the two heads in the water came back to me and I shook myself to clear it away. It couldn't have been the twins. There was no way they could have stayed under water that long. It was impossible as well as completely ridiculous.

I'd been confused by the swirling of the canoe.

I was dizzy and seeing things.

I was sick and frightened.

Anything but what my mind kept telling me was the truth.

I threw the useless paddle into the bottom of the canoe and headed for the safety of the channel.

As I moved along I kept looking around me and I had the unnerving sensation that something was watching me from the banks, but every time I whipped my head around for a look I saw nothing. Except for one time, when I was certain I saw a blur of movement, as if a figure had ducked down out of sight behind a large clump of reeds. I stopped paddling and stared for a long time but nothing untoward happened so I kept going.

I wanted to get out of the swamp as soon as was humanly possible.

When I got back to where I had left my bike Edie was sitting on the bank waiting.

'Hey, Chubby?' she said, but instead of her usual high-spirited look there was something curious and questioning in her eyes.

Instead of replying I hopped out of the canoe and started to pull it up out of the water. She came down to help me but I roughly tugged the canoe out of her grip.

'What's up with you?' she asked, trying to look hurt.

'Where are your sisters?'

'I don't know.'

'How'd you know where I'd be?' I said, dragging the canoe onto the trolley and securing it with the ockie straps.

'Your brother said you'd be here. We looked for you when we got back from the run, and he checked in the shed for the canoe. I just wandered around and looked for your bike. What's with all the aggression anyway?'

'You sure your sisters didn't tell you where I'd be?'

'What do you keep asking about my sisters for?'

'They were here, weren't they? In the swamp. Having a bit of a swim.'

'You're nuts,' she said, turning away and starting back along the track. 'My sisters can't swim, for starters, and Mum and Dad have banned them from going anywhere near the swamp. They reckon it's too dangerous.'

'You can say that again,' I called after her.

She turned around and screamed at me, 'IT'S TOO DANGEROUS!' And then started to run away along the track.

I stood there for a minute and watched her go.

She knew something, I realised. But what it was I had no idea. There was more there as well, a look way back in her eyes, and I thought I knew what it was.

Swampland

Edie was worried. She was worried about me.

And that, for some stupid reason, made me suddenly feel very happy.

7

I had to tell someone about what happened, but I didn't think my parents were likely to lend a sympathetic ear. It was a fairly strange thing to relate, after all.

'Hi Mum. Hi Dad. Hey, you know the twin girls next door? Well they've got something weird going on in the swamp. I'm not really sure what it is, though. There are all these candles on this old raft that I built with Max and Michael, and when you get really close to it there's an awful smell. All this strange foam stuff is floating around it as well. Oh yeah, and one more thing. The twins seem to be able to . . . well . . . live under water. Or at least stay under water for extremely long periods of time. And they like to chew up canoe paddles and scare the living crap out of anyone who happens to be in their vicinity. So, what do you reckon? Pretty crazy, huh? Shall we call the police or what?'

Fat chance.

The other thing about the whole situation was Edie. She had to have some idea about what the twins were up to, but how much I didn't know. I really didn't want to get on her wrong side or upset her, especially since we'd been getting on so well over the last couple of weeks. To be quite honest about it, I was more concerned about her reaction to me than I was about anything else. All that had really happened was that my canoe had been twirled about, and that wasn't anything to get all hoity-toity about, as my grandmother would say. The fact that I was scared to the point of going cross-eyed didn't seem to matter so much now that I was away from the situation.

And when it all came down to it, I really had no idea of what was happening back there in the swamp with the old raft. It was all just a little too strange for me and I needed another perspective.

Someone who wasn't quite as set in their ways as Mum and Dad tended to be.

Someone who would listen without sneering at me and thinking I'd just had a little too much sun or that my imagination was working overtime.

Naturally, I chose Zac.

When he finally stopped laughing my face was so red with embarrassment I thought it was going to explode.

He was whooping and wheezing like someone with half a chicken leg stuck in their throat, tears pouring down his face. I thought he was going to fall out of his chair.

Every time the laughter subsided he'd look up at me and the look on my face would start him off again.

If possible I would have curled up into a ball and hidden behind the couch like all the other discarded bits and pieces that no-one has any use for.

So when he did finally stop, I was not exactly in the mood for further discussion.

'I'm sorry, Marvin,' he spluttered. 'It's just so . . . so fanciful? Is that the word for it? I'm just not used to stories like that, especially from you. Hellspawn and

Hemlock are doing what in the swamp? Living under water and holding ceremonies on your old raft! Eating paddles and turning your canoe around in circles! Come on, Marvin, let's be serious for a minute. What's this really all about?'

'I told you,' I muttered, unable to look him in the eye. He laughed.

'It's about Edie, isn't it?'

'No.'

'There's a few hormones raging about in your system?'

'NO!'

'Hmmm?'

'Get stuffed, Zac.'

'Ooh, that sounds like a hormone speaking.'

'I'm sorry I said anything.'

'Did you really throw up?'

'No. I made that bit up. Come on, let's forget about it, I was probably just suffering from sunstroke or something.'

'Sunstroke?'

'Yeah, sunstroke.'

I started to walk off, trying as best I could to look angry and dignified at the same time, which didn't work. I had the feeling I looked more like a penguin with piles than an angry young man.

Zac let me get as far as the shed before he called out to me.

'Hey, come on Marvin, I'm sorry, all right? I didn't mean to laugh at you, but can you blame me? Really? How would you feel if someone came up to you with a story like that?'

He wheeled himself up next to me and I did my best possible imitation of an Easter Island statue.

'Look, I've apologised,' he continued, 'and I'm not going to keep on grovelling just to stroke your ego along a bit. If you want to show me this paddle, show away, otherwise let's drop it.'

So I showed him the paddle, and all of a sudden he wasn't laughing quite so much.

If I'd expected something to come of it all that night I was sorely mistaken. Zac was certainly impressed with the damage done to the paddle, and even though he'd never felt comfortable around the twins he had a lot of trouble accepting that the damage done to the wood was the work of a couple of ten-year-old girls.

He had even more trouble accepting the fact that they'd done the damage under water.

'What did Edie say about it all?' he asked as we went back inside the house.

'She reckons that the twins can't swim and that they're not allowed to go into the swamp. Their parents think it's too dangerous.'

'Well something's not right, then. I don't know about the swimming part but I see the twins coming out of the swamp all the time.'

'Yeah, I know.'

'But that doesn't mean anything in itself. I'm pretty sure lots of kids aren't allowed in the swamp, but that doesn't stop them. It certainly doesn't mean they chewed up your paddle.'

'But they did, Zac. I saw them.'

'You said you were really dizzy at the time. How can you be sure?'

'Why was I dizzy? Who did that to the canoe?'

'Sunstroke?'

I was about to answer him when Mum and Dad suddenly came rushing out to us, all flustered and nervous.

Zac took one look at them and said, 'It's Aunt Lisa, isn't it?'

Mum burst into tears.

Mum's sister had been dying for as long as I could remember and we'd had panic sessions before. But this time it looked like it was for real.

Aunt Lisa had been a smoker since she was about fifteen, and had been playing touch and go with lung cancer since her early thirties. A couple of times she'd got really bad and all her brothers and sisters had rushed down to Melbourne and sat around waiting for her to give up the ghost, but she'd come out of it, snapping and snarling at the doctors and cracking jokes to the waiting family members about vultures and dead meat.

This time was different, though. She was in a coma for starters and it didn't sound like she'd be making very many jokes about anything.

Mum was a wreck, and Dad—though doing his best to appear staunch and resolute—wasn't all that much better. They were leaving for Melbourne immediately and didn't know how long they'd be gone.

Dad gave Zac a couple of hundred dollars to take care of things like shopping and bills, and half an hour later we were seeing the two of them off in a taxi.

It all happened so quickly I was in a state of shock.

'Hope they catch that plane,' Zac said, turning around on the veranda and looking at me. 'They're cutting it very fine.'

'Yeah, they'll make it. You think she's going to die this time? I mean, she's been okay before.'

'Sounds like this one's fairly certain. I just hope she comes out of it long enough to know that everyone's there for her. But even if she doesn't wake up I think she'll know anyway.'

He looked at me closely.

'Hey, are you okay? You're looking a bit green around the gills.'

'I'm fine,' I said, bursting into tears.

Zac pulled me over so that I ended up sitting on his lap and hugged me into his shoulder, which I proceeded to soak. It was the way he used to hold me when I was little and I'd hurt myself, though in those days he wasn't permanently in a chair.

Any other time the thought of sitting on my brother's lap and crying into his shoulder would have embarrassed me beyond description, but right at that time I didn't give a stuff who saw me.

'It's all right,' he kept repeating. 'It's all right, it's all right.'

'I really liked Aunt Lisa,' I sobbed.

'She knows, Marvin, she knows.'

We sat like that on the veranda for what seemed like hours, until I finally calmed down and we went back inside to work out how we were going to arrange things over the next few days. Or until we knew what was going to happen down in Melbourne.

Zac and I had been left on our own before, so it really wasn't any big deal. I just wasn't all that happy about the circumstances.

Oddly enough, all thought of the incident in the swamp had gone right out of my mind.

That night I had the strangest dream.

To begin with I thought I'd woken up, because it felt like I was still in bed. But when I looked up the ceiling seemed to be made out of some sort of woven grass matting.

I tried to sit up but found that my arms seemed to be pinned down at my sides and I couldn't move my legs at all. It was at that stage I knew it was a dream, because I often dream of being pinned down. The situation, however, was a new one for me so I relaxed and waited for something to happen.

The fact that I knew it was a dream didn't stop it from scaring me half to death, though.

Firstly, I thought I smelled smoke.

Then the twins appeared from either side of me, their fat-lipped mouths spread wide in grins that showed their horrid peg teeth. I could feel saliva dripping onto my face and chest.

Then one of them—I don't know if it was Violet or Mauve—dipped her head down around the area of my stomach, and though I couldn't feel anything, I could tell by the look on the other's face that something particularly unpleasant was happening. I could also hear some pretty ghastly chewing sounds, which didn't help the situation any either.

What was worse, though, was the face of absolute glee on the watching twin, who kept looking at what was happening to my stomach and then back at me.

Every time she looked at me she nodded happily and seemed to whisper something, but I was unable to hear what she was saying.

Then the other twin looked up.

Her entire head seemed to be covered in blood, almost as if she'd had it right inside me, and in her mouth was something that looked like a liver. She was chewing on it vigorously, shaking her head from side to side, the way you see animals do in those boring TV documentaries.

That was when I started screaming my head off.

I screamed until Zac's shouting brought me back to reality.

8

'That was some doozey of a nightmare you had last night,' Zac said over breakfast. 'The way you were going on, I thought we'd been broken into or something. I'm amazed you didn't wake up the entire neighbourhood.'

I could still remember the dream with incredible clarity, so the fact that Zac had grilled up bacon for breakfast didn't appeal to me much.

When I'd finally come to my senses the night before, the first thing I did was grab at my stomach with both hands, half expecting to find a huge hole there. Naturally, there wasn't. But I could feel my heart going nineteen to the dozen and my sheets were soaked through with sweat.

At least I hoped it was sweat. I had to turn on the light to make sure.

Then I went in and calmed Zac down, who was bellowing his head off. I guess he feels kind of helpless when something happens at night, because it takes him a good ten minutes to get himself out of bed.

By the time I got to his room he was half into his chair already, a look of real panic on his face. When he saw I was all right he called me every name under the sun and then some, before he finally calmed down and let me help him get settled again.

His bed was a real mess because his bag had come loose while he was trying to get into his chair, so I had to fix all that up while he muttered and mumbled to me about juvenile fantasies and night sweats (I hadn't told him what I'd been dreaming, only that I'd had a nightmare).

After that I hadn't slept much at all.

'So what was the nightmare?' he continued.

'Oh, I don't remember now,' I lied. 'Probably something to do with Aunt Lisa.'

'Yeah, it happens.'

Zac looked fairly sad himself, and we continued our breakfast in silence, each away with his own thoughts.

When Edie appeared at the kitchen window we both jumped.

'Hi guys, where's the folks?'

'Melbourne,' Zac said around a mouthful of bacon. 'Gone to see our aunt.'

'That's great,' she went on. 'That mean you've got the house to yourselves?'

'Yeah, but we're not thinking of having any parties, if that's what you're going to suggest.'

'Parties! No. But I could come over and cook you dinner some night. How'd you like that?'

'Zac and I can cook,' I interjected.

'I didn't say you couldn't, Chubby. I just offered to help, that's all. You're not still all funny, are you?'

'Don't worry about Marvin,' Zac said quickly. 'He's just a bit upset. We both are. Our aunt's pretty sick and we're not sure how things are going to turn out.'

'Oh, sorry. I didn't mean to have a go at you, Chubby.'

'That's all right.'

There was an awkward pause for a minute, then Edie went on, sounding a bit strained, the way people tend to when they've just been told something unpleasant and are not sure how to act.

'So, are we running this morning?'

'Nah,' said Zac, 'we're just going to take it easy today. You know, hang around and wait for a phone call from Mum and Dad so that we know what's happening.'

'Okay then,' she said, relieved at having a reason to leave. 'Maybe tomorrow or something?'

'Sure,' said Zac. 'Tomorrow would be fine.'

'I'll see you then. And I'm sorry about your aunt, I really am.'

'Thanks Edie,' Zac and I said together.

'She's nice, just like her mum and dad,' Zac said after Edie had left. 'She's just trying to be friendly.'

Mr Tucker had been talking to Zac about a job in the advertising agency he ran, somewhere in the art department, where he'd be able to help with designing and putting together print ads and packaging and stuff. Zac had been really excited about it and had even started making inquiries about taking a graphic design course at the technical college.

'Yeah, I know,' I replied. 'I've just got a lot on my mind, that's all.'

He nodded.

'And by the way,' I continued, 'they're not her parents.'

'What?'

'They're all adopted. Mr and Mrs Tucker were friends of their parents. They died in an accident in America when Edie and the twins were really little. Their name used to be Fischer.'

'You don't say,' Zac said thoughtfully. 'What did their real parents do?'

'I think she said they were scientists or something.'

'Hmmm.'

'What's up,' I asked.

'Oh, nothing. The name Fischer seems to ring a bell, that's all, but I'm probably just imagining it.'

⁂⁂⁂⁂⁂
⁂⁂⁂⁂⁂

Not long after breakfast Zac said something about doing some shopping for dinner and took off, telling me to make sure I stuck around in case Mum or Dad called about Aunt Lisa. I didn't exactly relish the job of playing answerphone, but someone had to do it.

One of these days, I thought, Mum and Dad will catch up to the twentieth century and buy one of the damn things. Everyone else's parents had an answerphone, and some of the kids I went to school with even had mobile phones. The closest I'd ever come to modern technology was when I got a solar calculator, but that was only because it was some sort of give-away Dad had picked up at a conference. It looked like a white packet of matches until you flipped the lid. Then you had to hold it in direct sunlight for a while before it worked properly, which didn't exactly help when you were in a classroom trying to come to grips with an especially complicated maths problem.

'It's good for you to learn how to work things out for yourself,' Dad had said when I complained about the calculator, daring to suggest to him I'd do a lot better with one I could simply plug in or something. 'What would happen if we lost all the power in the world and there was no electricity for computers and calculators and things like that? If no-one knew how to do things without power-assisted machines we'd all just shrivel up and die, wouldn't we?'

I considered saying we could all survive quite happily by using batteries, solar power and the like, but I didn't think it was a good time to go shooting my mouth off, especially since Dad looked so righteous.

For most of the morning after Zac left I just hung around the house doing all those little things you can do to fill in time without really seeming to do anything: washing dishes, tidying our rooms and watching some of that really dumb morning television while trying to read one of my father's Ed McBain books, but I really couldn't get into it.

I'd got to the point where I was beginning to get more interested in Ernie and Denise than I was in the book when someone knocked at the window and I looked up to find Edie with her face pushed up against the pane so that her nose was all squashed to one side.

'Very, very attractive,' I said, sliding the window open so that she could climb inside.

'Why thank you, kind sir,' she replied, bouncing down onto the lounge beside me. 'It's so rare to find a gentleman these days. Especially one of such generous proportions.'

'Oh, give it a break, Edie. I've lost heaps of weight since we've all been running. Even Zac says so.'

'Well he's your brother, isn't he. He's supposed to say things like that, whether they're true or not.'

'Thanks.'

'Don't mention it.'

She sat there for a while staring straight ahead, then gave a sigh and reached over and took my hand. It felt like someone had given me an electric shock.

I froze.

'Relax, Marvin. I came here to make peace, not have another argument. How about a truce?'

'I didn't know we were at war.'

'You know what I mean.'

'Yeah, sorry.'

'What about this: If you stop asking ridiculous questions about my sisters, I'll stop making comments about your weight.'

'They weren't ridiculous questions, I was just curious, that's all, and I'd had a bit of a fright.'

She shook her head angrily.

'Stop being stupid, Marvin. You know exactly what I mean. I'm very close to Violet and Mauve. We have to be close, because we're really all we have. The Tuckers are nice and everything, they look after us, but we know they're not our real parents, no matter how much we talk about them as if they are. They make sure we're aware of our origins. Our real parents insisted on that. So I don't like anyone asking suspicious questions about my sisters. They're blood, and you know what they say about that.'

'What?'

'It's thicker than water.'

'Oh, right.'

'A truce then?'

'Okay, truce.'

We were still sitting there holding hands and watching the end of Ernie and Denise when Zac came home.

Instead of shopping bags, his lap was filled with what appeared to be library books, on top of which was a beige folder with papers spilling out. He gave us a sick sort of smile and said something about deciding to do some reading instead of the shopping and continued to roll straight past us into his bedroom.

He closed the door behind him and I thought I heard him lock it, though I couldn't really be certain because Ernie laughed at that moment, which would have been enough to drown out the sound of a Mack truck coming through the lounge room wall.

'Don't tell me your brother's gone all funny as well?' Edie said as the door closed behind him.

'No, he's fine,' I said, but I wasn't so sure. He'd looked quite guilty when he went past us, like he'd just been caught out at something sneaky.

Edie left not long afterwards and I had the rest of the day to myself. Zac stayed locked in his room, and every time I knocked and asked him if he wanted anything—like a sandwich for lunch, a cup of tea or if he felt like watching the cricket test on TV—he told me to leave him alone.

This was not like him at all, especially not wanting to watch the cricket. Zac had never been much of a book person, unlike myself, and I didn't know what to make of it. I figured he'd picked up some things on graphic design or the like to help him along with the job suggestion from Mr Tucker. He did have a habit of immersing himself completely when a subject took his interest, like the training for the Paralympics, so I left him to himself and spent the rest of the day in the shed repairing my damaged paddle.

I did quite a good job on it, even if I do say so myself, and had just finished painting it when Zac suddenly burst into the shed. He had never got used to opening doors after he was confined to the wheelchair, and he tended to take a bit of a run-up and charge through them. Most of the locks in our house were stuffed because of this (except for the one on his bedroom door, he'd always been very careful with that), and Dad had given up repairing them because Zac would just charge through them again. It was a sore point between the two of them, but one in which Zac had the upper hand.

'Where's that paddle?' he half-shouted at me. 'The one that looked like it was all chewed up?'

'There,' I said, proudly pointing at it as it swung from a wire hook in the ceiling.

The fresh red paint was still glistening and there were some spots on the concrete floor which I was about to wipe up with a turpentine-soaked rag.

Zac stared at it for a few seconds, his mouth hanging slightly open, then he dropped his head into his hands and groaned.

'What's the matter?' I asked. 'Haven't I done it right?'

Zac shook his head.

'No, there's nothing wrong with it. You've done a great job.'

'So what are you looking so depressed about?'

'Never mind.'

He wheeled himself back out of the door, and by the time I had cleaned up the paint drips and gone back inside the house his door was shut once again. When I put my ear to it I could hear him muttering to himself, but I couldn't make out what he was saying.

Whatever it was, he didn't sound too happy.

He told me all about it that night, while we were having dinner, and it put me right off my little lamb chops, which is about my favourite meal, so it will give you some idea of how unpleasant his theory turned out to be.

The kitchen was full of the sizzle of fat and the odour of steaming vegetables when Zac finally opened his door and rolled up to the table. He looked tired and preoccupied, and when I asked him how many chops he wanted he just shrugged and stared at his place at the table, which was so unlike Zac I immediately knew something major was on his mind.

We ate in silence for ten minutes or so before he pushed his plate away from him, still half uneaten, sighed and looked over at me.

'Marvin,' he said, rubbing his eyes and looking distinctly uncomfortable, 'there's something I have to tell you.'

'Uh huh.' I was concentrating on crunching chop tails between my teeth and thinking about how pleasant my morning had been with Edie.

'I've been down to the library and done some research.'

'You don't say.'

'Come on, Marvin, pay attention. This could be important.'

I put down my chop bone and smeared grease across my mouth with the back of my hand.

'I'm all ears,' I said, distractedly.

'I've found out a few things about Edie's parents. About what they did and the accident that happened in America.'

That got my complete attention.

'Go on, I'm listening.'

'You know how Edie told you her parents were scientists?'

I nodded.

'Well, did she happen to mention what branch of science they were interested in?'

I thought about it for a minute.

'No, she didn't say.'

'They were ichthyologists.'

'Ikky whats?'

'Ichthyologists. They did research into fish.'

That really made me pay attention.

'Yeah, she showed me one of her father's books a while back. It was about fish. All sorts of weird, creepy things that live in fresh water.'

'Her parents were pretty weird themselves. They had some rather odd theories and bent quite a few rules in their research, which is why they had to go to America. They were virtually thrown out of New Zealand.'

'Why?'

'They were doing some unpleasant experiments on animals.'

'What sort of experiments?' I was starting to feel very uncomfortable.

'It's a bit complicated, which is why I've had to spend so much time going through the books. They published quite a bit in science journals while they were still in New Zealand. At that time they were still fairly well respected, at the top of their field and everything. But then they started to go over the top.'

He stopped talking for a minute and scratched his head vigorously before continuing.

'I'm not even sure of this myself, but the essence of it is that they believed there was a way of making mammals breathe under water.'

'Oh no.' I was suddenly starting to feel very ill.

'It was all to do with genetics and cross-breeding and things, which is not a subject I know too much about. They actually had some success with rats. Not a lot, but they managed to get some to survive for a couple of hours. It's when they started to experiment with monkeys that everything got out of hand.'

I pushed my plate as far away as possible and sat back to hear all the ghastly things that had been in the back of my mind come to life.

'The church as well as the scientific community got into the act and condemned them outright. They were accused of tampering with nature, playing God, the whole box and dice, and the government cut off their funds. After that it's a bit hard to work out exactly what happened, but there was definitely a move to America. The trouble is, they didn't publish anything after that time, which makes me suspect they were working for something very heavy.'

'Heavy?'

'Yeah, like the military or something.'

'Oh, great, the American military. Really nice company to be keeping.'

'Exactly. Mind you, it's only a suspicion on my part. The only references I can find on the Fischers after they went to the States are newspaper reports on the accident. That's what started it all, because I remembered something about that, when you mentioned their name at breakfast this morning. There was a lot in the papers about it when I was a kid, and I can remember Dad reading it out to Mum over the table in the mornings. I don't know why it stuck in my mind all these years, but it did.'

'Tell me about the accident.'

'Well, this is another bit that gets strange. They couldn't really work out if it was an accident or not. The papers hint at the fact that it could have been done deliberately, by the Fischers themselves.'

'What could have been done deliberately?'

'The fire that burnt down their research facility. They both died in it. Edie and the twins were there at the time but were dragged out by the firemen. The twins were only a few days old.'

'I don't believe it.'

'Oh, that's not the worst part.'

I stared at him, waiting for it.

'The reason they survived was because Edie took the twins and hid from the fire inside a large tank of water.'

That's when I ran to the toilet and threw up.

9

Zac had a lot more to tell me, and after I'd finished disposing of dinner and composing myself we sat at the kitchen table for hours as he took me through it.

The more he told me, the more incredible it became.

And the more incredible it was, the more obvious it seemed.

Zac had even sorted out the part the missing pets played in the whole situation.

'Let's just say the Fischers had some success with their experiments,' he said.

'What sort of success?'

'With the twins. I mean I can't really be sure of this, but from what I've read and what you've told me about what's going on in the swamp, let's presume they have some sort of ability to survive under water.'

'They can definitely do that,' I agreed.

'Okay. So that means they have a degree of fish genes, though how much I have no idea.'

'They look like fish.'

'Yeah, and so does old Mrs Lupoff from the corner store, but I bet she can't breathe under water.'

'What about Edie?'

'I don't think Edie's part of this, though I think she

85

must have some idea of what's going on. She was born before they left New Zealand, and as far as I can work out they were only experimenting with animals at that stage.'

'Good.'

Zac grinned at me.

'You'd be pretty upset if she was part fish, wouldn't you? Maybe you ought to take her down the pool some day and really find out.'

'No thanks. Go on.'

'Well fish—all fish—are either hunters or scavengers. They prey on smaller fish and sometimes even their own kind.'

'Cannibals. How nice.'

'It's just part of their make-up, there's nothing they can do about it. And I reckon they're feeding themselves up for something. That whatever part of them is fish is taking over from the human part and making them do this, forcing them to behave like fish would.'

I swallowed loudly.

'Feeding themselves up for what?'

'I had to really think about that part, and do an awful lot of reading, but I think I've got it. You said the raft had all this foamy stuff around it.'

'Yeah, but it wasn't really like foam, more like sago or frogs' eggs or something.'

I suddenly realised what I had said. Zac nodded at me.

'That's right. Eggs. I think they're spawning.'

'No.'

'Yes.'

'NO!'

Zac just stared at me. I started to feel ill again. Then I thought I'd found a flaw in his argument.

'Hang on a minute! They'd have to have a male to spawn properly. They're both girls.'

'Not necessarily,' said Zac. 'There are quite a number of fish that can change sexes virtually as it suits them. They are males all their life until it comes time to spawn, then some of them simply switch over to being females. It's part of their survival mechanism. But there's a bit I found in the reports of the accident in America that seems really odd, and I thought at first it was just a mistake. Now I'm not so sure. Here, read this.'

Zac handed me a photocopy of an American newspaper article. It called Edie a hero for having the foresight to climb into the tank of water when the fire broke out in the laboratory, but it was the headline that really threw me.

I kept staring at it for ages, reading the words over and over because I just couldn't believe them.

5-YEAR-OLD GIRL SAVES TWIN BROTHERS FROM FIRE.

Sleep did not come to me very easily that night.

Neither Zac nor I could come up with a reason why the Tuckers had kept the twins disguised as girls, other than to confuse anyone who might be looking for them. And the only people who might do that had to be from America.

Which was not something we really wanted to think about, as it sounded too outrageous.

Mind you, twin boys disguised as girls who ate pets and spawned in the swamp was a bit much as well, but we had the facts and it was hard to ignore them.

We decided to call Officer Donleavy in the morning and give him an anonymous tip about the raft and how it related to the disappearing pets.

'Let the police work it all out,' Zac said as he wheeled off towards his bedroom at around one in the morning. 'That's what they're here for, after all, to sort out problems.'

I lay in bed thinking about everything we'd talked about. No matter what questions I'd come up with, Zac always seemed to have a theory, and they made sense, even down to the candles on the raft.

'They're confused, that's all. Their biology is making them do one thing, but you have to remember they're still part human, so they try and make sense out of it. They've turned it all into a ritual, sort of like primitive man did when he didn't understand his motivations; made it into a religious thing.'

It was all a bit highfalutin for my taste, and I don't profess to have understood a lot of it, especially the ritual bit, but when Zac talked about it it made sense.

Sleep finally came to me, but at what time I have no idea. It was filled with disturbing dreams, but the images were murky and without clarity.

I was instantly awake, however, when I heard Zac shouting.

'MAAAAARVIN! MAAAAARVIN!'

Racing down the hallway to his room I thought I saw movement out of the corner of my eye, a shape or shapes that scuttled off through the lounge room, but I was in too much of a hurry to pay attention. Zac's door was wide open and he was shouting at the top of his voice.

He sounded frightened, which was so unusual for Zac. I was close to panic.

His room looked like a bomb had hit it. The books and papers he'd brought from the library were ripped up and scattered about like confetti. The doors to his cupboards were almost off their hinges and his clothes were all over the room.

Worst of all, his wheelchair was on its side, the spokes torn out or buckled like they'd been hit by a truck.

I stopped in the doorway and stared, my mouth wide open and my breath coming in huge gulps. Then I realised I couldn't see Zac. His bed was just a tangle of sheets, the pillows ripped open and duck down drifting through the air.

'ZAC!' I shouted, rushing in through the door. 'ZAAAAC!'

'Over here, you moron,' came the reply from the other side of the bed.

He was on the floor, a jumble of arms and legs, trying to work his way out from underneath his bedside table.

'Well don't just stand there,' he snarled when he saw me. 'Help me into my chair.'

I managed to get him back on the bed.

'Sorry about the chair,' I said, when he finally looked over and saw the damage.

'Ugly, vicious little bottom feeders,' he muttered angrily.

'Who? What?'

'The twins.'

'They were here?'

'Yeah, they were here all right. I woke up and they were over in the corner of the room with the books I'd brought from the library. They were looking through them and whispering to each other. When they saw I was awake they just went berserk. But the really creepy thing was they did it silently, no shouting or hurling things around, just taking them from one place, ripping them up and then placing them on the floor. It was like watching a silent movie. I thought they were going to kill me, but I think they just wanted to give me a fright.'

'Looks like they succeeded.'

He looked across at me and broke into a grin.

'Yep, they scared the legs right out from under me.'

'That's not funny.'

'Yes it is. But I tell you what isn't. They kept repeating it while they were quietly trashing the room, just before they heaved me out of bed . . . "you're too late, you're too late, the moon's out, the moon's out, you're too late".'

'Too late for what?'

'I think the eggs are about to hatch. Look outside.'

Through the curtains I saw a gigantic full moon. I looked back at Zac, a puzzled expression on my face.

'Most fish breed in cycles,' he said. 'Cycles related to stages of the moon.'

'We have to stop them,' Zac said, with absolute finality.

'Why?'

'Probably for the same reason their parents tried to wipe them out before. What they've created is horrible. It could affect the entire balance of nature on this planet. It's unnatural. Imagine what would happen if they got out of the swamp? Fish breed in millions, Marvin. Can you imagine what millions of pet-eating Hellspawns and Hemlocks would be like? And you can be pretty certain they won't stick to small animals. It would be like piranha learning to live on land.'

'Let the police do it.'

'You think they're going to believe us? Don't be stupid.'

'But we can tell them it's to do with the pets, like we planned. They'll have to do something then.'

'But not until morning. Don't argue with me, Marvin. Just drag me out to the shed.'

'Then what are you going to do? Shout over the fence at them?'

'No, oh smart one, you're going to put me in your canoe and you're going to pedal the both of us down to the swamp.'

'It's the middle of the night!'

'We'll use Dad's flashlight.'

'You're nuts.'

'And you're my brother. So let's go.'

***

I did what he asked, nearly breaking my back dragging him through the house and across the yard, but the morning exercise with the bike must have been paying some dividends because I was still breathing when we got there. Zac started dragging himself around the shed, pulling things out of cupboards and muttering to himself.

While he was occupied with his arrangements, I snuck back inside and called the police station.

Donleavy wasn't there, which was only natural since it was after three in the morning by this time, but the duty officer said he could get him a message if it was an emergency.

'Just tell him Zac and Marvin are in the swamp. They know what's been happening to the pets. And tell him to hurry.'

The voice on the other end of the phone didn't sound very happy, but he said he'd talk to whoever was in charge.

I hung up and dashed back out to the shed. Zac was propped up in the corner holding Dad's huge flashlight and a can of petrol.

'Where the hell have you been,' he snarled.

'Having a nervous wee. Are you sure you want to do this?'

'Just get me in the canoe and strap it on the back of the bike.'

That sounded a lot easier than it was, and it took me a good twenty minutes to do what he wanted. Zac kept urging me to hurry, but there's only so much one-and-a-half bodies can do in a small shed in the middle of the night.

Eventually we were ready and I pedalled unsteadily out of the shed doors, my legs straining with the unaccustomed weight. Behind me Zac kept saying 'Faster, faster'.

He sounded both excited and angry at the same time.

I hoped the message had got through to Donleavy.

10

I don't remember a lot about the ride down into the swamp, and I think the reason for that is because it took so much out of me. Zac weighs quite a bit, and with him sitting in the back of the canoe it took every ounce of strength I had to build up enough momentum to get the whole box and dice moving.

Stopping, however, is crystal clear to me.

The bike stopped okay, but because of the weight in it the canoe didn't, simply snapping the ockie straps and riding up into the rear wheel of the bike. I was thrown off to one side as the canoe smashed through the wheel, totally destroying the entire rear end of my only mode of transport. When I looked up from where I'd fallen, Zac was still sitting in the canoe, which was embedded in the bike, holding the flashlight and petrol can and looking across at me as if I was the lowest form of life on earth.

'Haven't you ever heard of easing the brakes on?' he said, the disgust obvious in his voice. 'Come on, let's get on with it.'

It took me another twenty minutes to remove the canoe from the remains of the bike and to drag it the couple of metres down to the water. Zac insisted on taking the rear position.

'I'm stronger than you, that's all,' he said. 'I can paddle a lot faster in case we get into trouble.'

'Trouble?'

'Take the flashlight and let's get going.'

So with myself as guide and torch bearer and Zac propelling the canoe along with strong, sure strokes of the paddle, we left the safety of the land and entered the waterways.

A swamp at night is one of the eeriest things you could ever hope to experience, full of noise and movement one second, deathly silent the next.

There was a light breeze blowing, so all the trailing vines and overhanging branches moved like they were alive, and every now and then a large frog would splash into the water, creating ripples which I would carefully inspect with the flashlight. The light also had the habit of picking up the eyes of creatures hidden in the bushes and reeds watching our progress, so it was like we were travelling through a particularly creepy horror house from some supernatural sideshow.

It was so different in the dark that I had difficulty knowing exactly where we were, so a couple of times we got lost and had to retrace out path.

Every time this happened, Zac would mutter angrily at me, saying 'Get your act together, this isn't a game'.

Then, almost as if by accident, we broke through a stretch of reeds and found ourselves floating on Lake Marvellous.

Directly across from us we could see the raft lit up like a stage by all the candles. Its reflection stretched out across the waters, flickering slightly as the breeze stroked the candle flames. Everything looked calm and peaceful.

At least that's what I thought.

We sat in the now stationary canoe and watched for a few minutes, then I heard Zac swear under his breath.

'What?' I said, turning quickly, which wasn't a good idea because it made the canoe rock violently.

'Steady! Take it easy. I really don't fancy a dip tonight, thank you.'

'Sorry.'

'Now, really casually, and without panicking, I want you to turn the light down so that it's shining into the water alongside the canoe.'

'What makes you think I'll have a reason to panic.'

'I don't know yet, but there's something not quite right about the water. It seems sort of . . . I don't know . . . alive?'

Gulping loudly, I did what he asked.

At first, I didn't think there was any problem. The water looked its normal murky green colour, except more so because of the surrounding darkness and the unnatural illumination of the flashlight.

Then I thought I was seeing tadpoles, because the section of water I was lighting suddenly came alive with wrigglers which were a centimetre or two long.

The water was black with them.

Well, not quite black. Black and silver, actually, because the wrigglers all had a silver patch on their backs, and when I looked closely I could see that their eyes protruded from the sides of their heads.

They seemed to be attacking the light, rushing around in a frenzy, almost making the water boil with their movement.

I looked up at Zac.

'They've spawned,' he said. 'We'd better hurry.'

I began to feel a strange vibration through the sides

of the canoe and I realised it was the wrigglers bumping into it as they thrashed around us.

'They seem kind of excited,' I said as I jammed the flashlight into the front of the canoe so that it shone out before us like the single beam from a train.

I took up the extra paddle.

'Yeah,' said Zac. 'They're probably hungry.'

'No wonder you don't want to take a dip.'

※※※※※※

We cautiously crossed the lake until we were quite close to the raft, where the light from the candles continued to waver and dip; but it wasn't the breeze that was making the light move, it was what was happening around the raft.

The water was alive with the wrigglers, so thick with them it appeared like a black, seething stew. The sound of them smashing into the canoe was now quite audible, almost like rain on a tin roof. I could feel their vibration right through me, and it was unnerving to think of all those hungry black and silver bodies just millimetres away from my skin.

My skin, in fact, was crawling.

I was trying very hard not to think about what would happen if we overturned.

As we reached the raft I suddenly heard that cry, the weird ululation I'd heard the last time I was on Lake Marvellous, the one that had turned the twins away from the canoe.

It came out of the darkness behind the raft, much louder now that we were so close. I almost screamed in response, and behind me I heard Zac let out a loud grunt of surprise.

'What the hell is that?' he shouted at me.

'I have no idea,' I replied, 'But I heard it the last time I was here. It's got something to do with the twins.'

'It's Edie.'

'What? No way. She's not a part of this. I won't believe it.'

'Fine, have it your own way. We can argue about that later. Hold on to the raft for a minute.'

'I'm not touching that.'

'HOLD THE RAFT! NOW!'

Grabbing it with one hand, I steadied the canoe with the other, undecided as to what would be worse: whatever was behind the raft or having to face Zac's anger.

I heard him unscrew the top of the petrol can and the steady glug, splash, glug, splash, glug of the liquid pouring into the lake. The smell of petrol became overpowering and I became even more nervous at the thought of sitting in a steadily spreading pool of flammable liquid while so close to naked flames.

'Is this a sensible thing to be doing?' I asked, a definite quaver in my voice.

'Push off,' was Zac's reply, and I heard the sound of the petrol can being dropped into the water. 'That should fix the little aqua-maggots.'

We both used the paddles now, ploughing through the water with every bit of energy we could muster, the canoe almost rearing out of the water with the force of it. Within seconds we were half way back across the lake. Looking back I could see the petrol spreading out from the raft, an oily slick that seemed to follow the canoe. It was obviously upsetting the wrigglers, because I could see them leaping from the water in the pathway of reflected light.

I saw a blur of movement at the back of the reed cave as a large object crashed out of the reeds and into the water. The raft rocked wildly and for a second I thought the candles would overturn into the water.

'Damn,' exclaimed Zac. 'Give me the flashlight. Quickly.'

I tossed it to him and he drew his arm back as if to throw it.

Just then the water behind him erupted and the twins launched themselves at Zac, one of them grabbing his arm and the other landing in his lap. The flashlight dropped into the lake as he hauled the one holding his arm into the canoe with him. They were squirming and thrashing about, hissing and spitting like a bizarre cross between landed fish and feral cats. While one struggled with Zac, making the canoe rock violently, the other turned towards me, its eyes glowing unreally.

'Maaaarrrrvin,' it hissed as it crawled wetly towards me.

I reacted without really thinking. Swinging around, I held the paddle in both hands and used it like a baseball bat. It connected with the advancing twin's face and made a sound like a watermelon hitting a footpath.

Without a sound, it toppled backwards over the side of the canoe and disappeared under the water.

There was a second's pause as the other twin looked down at where its other half had gone, then it gave a wail and slithered over the side, Zac's paddle hitting the water just as it went under.

'Damn, missed him,' he snarled.

He leaned even further out of the canoe and grabbed the bobbing flashlight.

'CAREFUL,' I shouted.

The last thing I wanted now was for us to end up in the lake as well.

As Zac sat back upright I noticed he was bleeding from both hands and around his left shoulder where the twin's teeth had made contact.

He threw the flashlight with all his strength.

Time seemed to slow as it travelled in an arc through the air, its beam, still shining brightly, illuminating the paperbarks and reeds and briefly catching the oily water which still seethed with furious wrigglers.

Then it hit the raft dead centre, toppling candles on all sides, and the raft and water exploded with an enormous *WHOOSH!*

I had never seen anything like it. I froze as a wall of flame about three metres high travelled out from the raft across the water, only stopping about a paddle's length from the canoe. The heat from it blasted past my face, taking my eyebrows with it, and making my eyeballs feel like they were on the point of boiling.

'PADDLE!' screamed Zac, and my arms came back to life in a whirl of terrified movement.

All around the lake the dry reeds were bursting into flame, huge explosions that accompanied us on either side as we fled from the source of the fire. I hoped we'd make it back to the channel before the fire outdistanced us and cut off our escape.

Zac was laughing hysterically and shouting 'Gotcha, gotcha' with each stroke of his paddle. I think I was simply going 'Aaaahhhhh, aaaahhhhh' every time I let out a breath, which wasn't all that often.

Looking back over my shoulder I could see the section of water where the twins had disappeared was now covered with flames. In the brilliant orange light it looked like it was boiling. I preferred not to think about what was happening under the surface.

We made it to the channel with only seconds to

spare, the place we entered through suddenly closing off with flames just after we got inside. I realised then that being inside a thin channel with fire racing along the banks was not an ideal situation, and I seemed to increase my paddling speed even more, though how that was possible I have no idea.

'Keep going,' Zac gasped from behind me, 'we're going to make it. Keep going.'

I paddled with every ounce of strength I had.

The air was suddenly shattered by the strange cry once again, then a figure reared up out of the water directly in front of the canoe. With a wild shriek I dropped my paddle and lurched backwards, crashing into the middle support with my back. It felt like being stabbed with a shovel, the pain surging up and down my body in a wide swathe.

Zac grabbed me roughly by the shoulders and pushed me back up again, but all I could do was lurch forward and groan. Then the canoe slammed into something and stopped dead.

I lifted my head and stared straight into Edie's eyes, which were anything but friendly.

She was holding the prow with both hands, her hair slicked back and dripping and her lips peeled back over her pointed teeth. Her eyes were thin slits of total rage.

'HIT HER!' Zac shouted from behind me, but I was too stunned and sore to do anything.

I just stared at Edie, who snarled back at me, no sign of recognition in her face at all.

'Not you,' I said, weakly, and at the sound of my voice her face distorted hideously, as if speaking itself was an attack, and she twisted her hands and everything in the canoe ended up in the water.

From this point on, things became very blurred for me.

I have memories, but they are all jumbled up and distorted, and if I take any of them separately they make little sense. The nurses say that it is the result of shock, but I'm not so sure. I think that things happened just the way they appear to me, and that it's life itself that's distorting them by trying to make everything rational.

I can remember being under water with my lungs screaming for air. At one stage it seemed like I had surfaced inside a cave of some sort, but I think I'd just come up underneath the overturned canoe. There were also a lot of hands, some trying to pull me down and others trying to push me away. And everything happened either in total silence or within a huge roaring of noise that seemed so loud it should have left me permanently deaf, which I am not.

At one stage I know the fire was burning on both banks of the channel, and I have this image of Edie standing waist-deep in the water, flames in her hair and running across her arms, her mouth wide open and screaming at me, her mouth an open hole of either pure hate or pure pain, I'm not sure which.

But what I can't work out is if she was going back into the water or coming out of it. I had to be looking at her from the bank, otherwise I couldn't have been looking down on her, but how I got there I have no idea.

Also, Zac was there with her, just his head and shoulders showing above the water.

The picture I have is of his arms around her waist as if he was either holding her back or she was pulling him forward.

I can also remember the sound of sirens far off in the distance, and then everything is swallowed by the deepest shade of black that I have ever seen.

11

I woke up in the hospital, my parents anxiously waiting beside the bed.

Donleavy had got me out of the fire, getting himself badly burnt in the process. It appears that the message got through after all.

The fire wiped out the entire swamp, getting so hot that the water itself was boiling at one stage. The paperbarks and reeds were mostly tinder dry, so there was little chance of stopping it once it got started. Luckily, the fire engines that arrived managed to contain it within the general area of swamplands, so no private property was destroyed. The highway, however, was closed for some time and those houses that run close to the swamp's edge have, according to my parents, a scorched, too-long-in-the-sun kind of appearance.

It seems the council is now talking of filling the whole area with sand and reclaiming it for housing.

As for Zac, Edie and the twins, no trace of them has ever been found. They searched for days, dragging what little there was left of the waterways and going over the scorched ground for clues, but they keep saying nothing could have got out of there alive.

Rumour has it that the fire got so hot they were

burnt away completely, but I'm not so sure.

I'm not sure of anything these days.

I have the strangest feeling that they may not be dead, no matter what the evidence suggests to the contrary. There are so many unanswered questions. How did I get up on the bank? Zac certainly couldn't have done it, and I'm pretty sure I didn't do it myself. And was Edie pulling Zac out of the water or was he trying to hold her back?

There is a part of me that believes that whatever was human in Edie finally won out over what was not, and in the end she chose to help us when she realised she could no longer help the twins.

Maybe there was a way out of the swamp, some underwater channel or something that they followed. I don't know. But I'll find out some day.

For some strange reason, the nurses are calling me a hero, saying Zac and I went into the fire to rescue Edie and the twins, and I haven't said anything yet to dissuade them.

I need the time to think. To think about getting out.

So far, the doctors have kept the police away from me, saying I am still deeply in shock and unable to answer questions coherently.

I'm not coherent because nothing makes sense to me.

But one thing I do know is that some of the voices I hear arguing with the doctors about getting in to talk to me have American accents, and they don't sound very happy.

Their shapes are large and threatening through the opaque glass door of my room.

It's them I don't want to talk to, because I fear they know the truth.

And the truth—whatever it may be—is not something I'm quite ready for just yet.

So when it gets dark, I'm gone.
And I'm not coming back.